# PLANNING FOR NICKIE

---

## HOLIDAYS IN HADLEY SPRINGS
### BOOK TWO

## TASHA HACKETT

For Mom, who never let me
sit around and spout lies about "can't."

1

———

## MARK

SATURDAY, DECEMBER 23

Each year when I review my handwritten vision and life goals, I skip over one: *Get married by thirty*. I can't play that game anymore with my twenty-ninth birthday staring me in the face. I've got fifty-three weeks until the big 3-0.

Therefore, holiday break or not, before the second chirp of my four a.m. alarm, I vault out of bed, smash the silver snooze button, then click the alarm off. As planned, I'm now across the room and fully awake. My feet are silent on the carpet as I store my earplugs, straighten the bedcovers, then throw on a hoodie and shorts. After a quick scan of the room, I grab my work backpack and ease open the door to my borrowed bedroom. Soft blankets of noise from the sound machines in the kids' rooms greet me along the hall.

My cousin Diana and her husband, Nathan Weston, are hosting the family Christmas this year in middle-of-nowhere Hadley Springs, Nebraska. By the time I get to the kitchen, I know I'll need to return for pants. It's too cold in this house for gym shorts.

Diana turns from the sink and swallows a scream when she catches sight of me across the kitchen. "What the heck, Mark?" Diana whispers. "What are you doing up at four?"

"Sorry." I chuckle under my breath. "I'm off to work. This is the best time before your crazy house wakes up."

"God bless you. I just put Jack back down. You should have a couple hours, but they won't sleep in because they know you're here. You'll have until six at least."

"Yeah, and Cordy's asleep on the couch."

Diana pulls an egg carton from the fridge. "She was working on her phone when I came out at midnight."

"Jack again?" I take the eggs.

She grabs heavy cream, a package of diced ham, and cheddar cheese. "Actually, the midnight disturbance was Lisa. She wandered into our room with a story about tigers under her bed. Set those here." She nods to the counter.

"What are we doing?" The kitchen is lit by the under-cabinet lights along the floor. It's five after four, and she's arranging breakfast ingredients like it's perfectly normal. I was banking on having the quiet house to myself this early.

"Oh, nothing much. Throwing together an egg bake before I go to bed. I meant to do this yesterday. Here, get yourself some coffee, I'll be out in a minute. Where do you need to work?"

"The table is fine." I take the offered mug and set it under the single-serve coffee maker. By the time I've returned with sweatpants, my coffee is almost done, and Diana has cracked a dozen eggs directly into a glass baking dish. She whips them with a fork, tosses in cheese, ham, and a splash of cream. In one trip, she stores everything back in the fridge and finds a bag of tater tots from the freezer. She rips the bag open and dumps the whole thing on top and spreads them around with two hands.

"You're a whiz with that." I gather the spices—salt, pepper, garlic, onion flakes—and quietly return them to their rack along the wall. "You made family breakfast in the time it takes to brew a cup of coffee."

"Thanks. I guess I ought to know a thing or two after all these years." She pops a plastic lid on the dish and slides it into the fridge. "Well, good night."

"Night." The time is mine again. My favorite two hours of the whole day, and I don't have a single book to edit this week. I successfully finished my end-of-year deadlines early to make sure I'd have the extra time to plan out the elusive "to-do" that's haunted my life goals list for five years.

Coffee, notebook, and pen in hand, I settle at the kitchen table to review my life from years past. Halfway down the details of my ten-year vision, I stumble over that same sentence: *Get married by thirty*.

It's important. I want this for myself. I want kids, I want a family, and I look forward to making it a reality.

Before now, it was neither the most urgent nor important while I threw my efforts into *Establish Career*. Check! I've been sitting comfortably at Lakeview Publishing for three years, so there's nothing drastic I need to change for that. I'm up for another promotion anytime now. Believe me, I put in the work to get here, and I'm grateful I ground out those long weeks as a single man. As the most productive and disciplined editor at my publishing house, it makes sense that I've waited this long to find love.

Fifty-three weeks should be plenty of time to find a wife. One week to plan, fifty-two to execute.

I skim over my original vision, the clear picture of what I want. By thirty-five I have two kids, my wife and I enjoy evening swims in our backyard Arizona pool, and we've just celebrated our fifth wedding anniversary with a two-week tour of Italy with the kids and their nanny. Everyone should have a nanny. I twist my lips in a smirk. Diana is a power-house of a mother—in the best possible way—but I don't see anything wrong with hiring help. Preferably one who also bakes, sings lullabies in multiple languages, and knows CPR. But I'm flexible.

In my perfect plan, Mrs. Brader, my lovely wife, works part-time, oversees the house, volunteers at church, and likes to jog and workout with me a few times a week. The details I've put here still align with what I want.

May God bless my efforts this year. I write Proverbs 16:3 in my notes. *Commit your work to the Lord, and he will establish your plans.*

I turn a new page and think about my tasks for this year. If I'm introduced to Future-Wife in the next two months, we could be engaged by October for a winter wedding. When I return to Phoenix in a couple days, I'll begin asking my friends for introductions. Two dates a week... that's eight candidates by the end of January. It's a sure start. I nod, satisfied. It's a perfect plan.

In bold letters I title the top of the page, *Project: Find a Wife.*

## 2

## MARK



Cordy has all six of her nieces and nephews crowded around her on the couch. It's pretty awesome. These kids won the jackpot with the best family. Aunt Cordy. Then me, Uncle Mark—even if I'm technically a cousin.

I've been hiding in the kitchen for a few more minutes while I brew another cup of coffee. *Project: Find a Wife* is mind-mapped, outlined, timelined, and everything else I can do from here. The next and most important item on today's agenda is to play with the kids: Lauren, Landon, Leo, Lance, Lisa, and Jack. I love Arizona, but blizzard walks are in short supply and today is a perfect day for that adventure.

After pushing my notebook to the center of the table, I stretch and spy through the arched entry between kitchen and living room.

Jack and Lisa crowd Cordy's lap. The twins, Leo and Lance, squish into the corner beside her with Landon on her other side. Her feet are further trapped by Lauren leaning against her legs on the floor. They're midway through a Christmas edition of everyone's favorite baking show.

I take another sip of coffee before announcing my presence. "Morning, family."

"Mark!" A chorus of shouts drowns the TV. Leo's elbow knocks the side of Cordy's face when he leaps from the couch. "Mark! Mark, Mark, Mark!" They're like yapping dogs. Jack whimpers in Cordy's lap as she pauses the show.

I suck in a breath, lift my mug above the mayhem, and raise a hand against the mob. "Stop."

I've played a version of "Uncle Mark Says" with these kids since they were babies and have them well-trained. They love it, and I love how less anxious I am with kids who aren't squabbling. I nod in approval and speak as a commanding officer. "Line up."

They do, but I lift an eyebrow at their haphazard line.

"No, in order of height. No talking." And they do. Ten-year-old Lauren, then Landon and the twins. Toddler Lisa gets stuck trying to place herself between the boys and they forcefully shove her to the end of the line. She giggles, blond curls bouncing with her excitement. This game is the best.

"Hmm." I'm very stern as I inspect the line, knowing how to play my part with the right amount of authority without crushing any spirits. They willingly obey because they know something fun is coming.

"Jump three times. Spin in a circle. That's two circles, Lance. Enough. You may give me a high-five, but if you spill this coffee on her new carpet, you will make your mother cry and nobody wants that for Christmas."

I walk down the line accepting their high-fives as if taking tickets for a show and lower my voice to a near whisper before my announcement. "You're going to get dressed as quietly as possible—like sneaky secret agent ninjas—because if you wake your parents our whole day is ruined. Once you're dressed we'll go for a walk to look at the snow... and maybe I'll buy you donuts." I hold a finger to my lips. "On your mark, get set, go!"

Cordy sighs dramatically from the living room, her red hair caught in a terrible excuse of a bun. There may not even be a ponytail hidden in there. At this point it looks like a rodent had a dance party and the whole thing is one massive knot. "Here." She plops Jack on his back on the carpet. "Watch this one while I pee."

I stroll over and stare at the baby kicking his legs. "Can he have donuts?"

"What?" Cordy turns to me in shock. I take it that's a hard no.

"Kidding," I lie. Babies don't get donuts. Noted. Jack has teeth though, so I don't see what the big deal is.

Cordy backs away slowly, as if I can't be trusted to watch a pudgy, tiny human for thirty seconds. "Just... sit there. I'll be right back."

A *bing!* catches my ear, and I see her phone left on the floor. I settle on the edge of the couch and unlock her lifeline.

Gilbert: Oh, the weather outside is frightful...

Oh, hello! This must be the landlord she's refused to tell me anything about. I swipe down and, holy cow, there are hundreds of messages between the two of them. I quit trying to find the beginning of their thread and start reading.

Cordelia: Dearest Gilbert. I'm ASTOUNDED at your lack of faith in my "I'm not home" knowhow.

Gilbert: What if he's coming for the eggnog pie?

Cordelia: You ate the rest of it last night. I was going to make you another one, but I forgot. You want another one?

Gilbert: I do love a good eggnog pie.

Cordelia: HE'S COMING OVER HERE!

Gilbert: He must know someone's home. Did you stash the car?

Cordelia: I don't have time for your prattle. You'd prattle all day long if someone didn't put a stop to your nonsense. What does this look like to you? Chitchat around the water cooler? Swapping stories around the campfire??? We have a SITUATION. I'm telling you there's a strange man here that I've never seen before and it's sus. SUS I tell you.

Gilbert: What's your plan?

Cordelia: Text you, obv, and hide.

Gilbert: I'm not home.

Cordelia: OMG GILBERT IF YOU WERE HOME YOU'D DEAL WITH THIS AND I WOULDN'T BE TEXTING YOU.

Gilbert: Together now: Deep breath in.

Cordelia: *GIF of Rapunzel hiding in a pyramid of her own hair.*

I skim through dozens more texts filled with GIFs, flirting, Cordy's drama, and Gilbert's surprisingly effective crisis coaching. No wonder she's called me less the past couple weeks. Gilbert is supportive.

"Hey!" Cordy yanks the phone away. "Snoop. How'd you know my passcode?"

I was so engrossed in the Cordy-Gilbert saga that I didn't even hear her return. "I could tell you, but then I'd have to kill you."

"You're the worst." She punches my arm. Like a girl.

I raise my mug as the coffee sloshes over my fingers. "Ow! Coffee!" I think she was actually trying to hurt me, but she has the muscles of a Barbie. So, none. Coffee on the carpet would still be a problem. "Watch it." I wipe my fingers on my black sweatpants. "It's not my fault you've used the same four numbers since middle school."

I tap the side of my head and click my tongue. A text comes through her phone, and I've lost her. Her neck turns a blotchy red as guilt covers her features. She clears her throat and holds the phone to her ear.

Avoiding my gaze, she puts on a show of not caring what I think. Which is hilarious for how nervous she's acting. Gilbert must have answered, because a cheesy grin transforms her face the moment before she walks away.

Bambi's owl had it right. She's twitterpated. One hundred percent.

"Is everything okay? Shouldn't you be on a plane?" Her voice fades as she disappears into the kitchen.

I look at Jack, who's flipped to his stomach and starting to fuss. I find my key ring in my pocket and toss it to him. He startles when it rattles in front of his face, but then wiggles the few inches across the carpet to grab it. He likes it.

Jack investigates the rubber emblem in the shape of Arizona and chews on the fob for my office while I sing for him. "Cordy and Gilbert sittin' in a tree, K-I-S-S-I-N-G. First comes love, then comes marriage, then comes the baby in a baby carriage." Jack's not impressed with my singing.

I chuckle at the blank expression on the kid's face. I'm glad Cordy's happy though. Sure, I think it's a little soon after her breakup with Shaun to be dating again, but Shaun was completely wrong for her. From what I've heard from Cordy the past couple weeks, Gilbert appears to know what he's about. And these texts confirm my suspicions. He's into her.

Not that I'm any kind of relationship expert. But I hated seeing Cordy try to be somebody she's clearly not, when I know how wonderful she is. Any man is stupid who doesn't appreciate that.

Cordy paces back and forth in the kitchen, and I wave each time she casts furtive glances my way. "Sure," she says. "Anything else?" Cordy tugs on the collar of her shirt. "Okay. Be safe."

She stares at me, or through me, then downs a gulp of coffee. Before I get a chance to poke fun at her crush, the kids have returned—and they are not quiet.

Diana enters with Lisa holding her hand. "Morning. Lisa says Mark's taking everyone for donuts. Hey, when did Jack wake up? And why is he chewing on—Mark, is that your key fob?"

"Yeah." I hope it's waterproof. "He stole it from me."

"Alright. I'll have eggs and sausage ready when you get back." She finds a rubber giraffe under the coffee table and replaces the keys. "Cordy, you going with the gang?"

I return to the kitchen, dodging around the kids, who dig through a mound of snow gear. "She is."

"I am?" Cordy tries to punch me again, and I block her hand and yank her mess of a bun to the side. "Ow, don't touch me, jerk."

"Get your shoes on." I look through the coat rack and find Nathan's coveralls and boots. "I'll be ready in forty-five seconds."

Diana and Cordy bicker about the weather. It's two blocks. We're not taking Jack, and they can always come back if it's cold. I interrupt, "It's only twenty-seven degrees. We'll be fine. Help me with that baby wrap thing for Lisa." It's a contraption that keeps the kid in place, but takes an engineering degree to install. The two women wrestle two-year-old Lisa onto my back which gives the boys enough time for their own wrestling match in the front yard. "Hurry up, I'm sweating."

"Quit fussing." Diana secures the last buckle. "I'm trusting you to bring them all home in one piece. All six of them."

Cordy scoffs, knowing she's included in the list of kids. Once outside, the air is refreshing and a relief against my overheated body from the coveralls. It's fantastic. I love holidays. Surrounded by family. Clean air. Great food.

On an exhale I confess, in case Cordy didn't already know, "I read all your texts. Forget everything I've said the past two weeks. That's who you need to go after."

She throws her hands in the air, ever dramatic. "I've never gone after a man. That's pathetic." The snow blows thick around us. The sun is muted and white. There is no sky. White, white, white everywhere.

"Why?" I turn and count the kids. One, two, three, four, five. But the twins are lagging behind. "Come on, boys! Stay with us." The boys launch to their feet and run with arms twirling until they're slipping and sliding beside us.

I repeat the question, "Why?"

Cordy usually tells me everything. It's annoying that she's not right now. "It's pretty obvious if he's not interested."

Maybe, but not in this case. "And this Gilbert isn't interested?"

"The first day I moved here, I overheard John asking Gilbert if he could ask me out. Ew! Right? Like he needed permission? What a weird thing! Then, I thought maybe it was because Gilbert and John had talked about me before, and maybe Gilbert was planning to say something, but John was... I don't know. Then Gilbert said he didn't have time for a girlfriend. So, that's been clearly stated. Anyway, I don't want to go shoving myself where I'm not wanted, and what if I really hurt John's feelings because I like Gilbert better than John? I don't want that."

"You're not responsible for everyone's feelings."

"But shouldn't I attempt to give John a try? John's a really nice guy."

"Do you ever listen to the stupid things you say?" I shake my head in disgust and adjust the strap around my waist. I would hate for a girl to go out with me for any of the reasons stated. "We're not syrups at a coffee shop or flavors at an ice cream parlor. You're not obligated to give anyone a try."

"John is really nice."

"You're being an idiot." There's someone who obviously likes her, and she's whining about hurting another guy's feelings, who doesn't even have the guts to do anything about it? Heck, no.

"You're a real friend, Mark. Super glad you're here." Cordy increases her speed and marches ahead of me. She's annoyed, but she'll get over it. "Why don't you just mind your own stinking business?"

"Why are you mad?" I laugh while striding beside her. She's so easy to read. "Methinks the lady doth protest too much."

"It's swell hanging out with you. I always feel better about myself when you're around. A load of encouragement, that's you."

She's annoyed because I'm making her admit what she already knows. "Tell me you don't have feelings for Gilbert."

"Next time you're paying full price for an Uber."

Not likely. Cordy loves being useful. I clear my throat, knowing I'm on to something. "Tell me you don't have feelings for Gilbert."

"Gag. *Feelings for.*" Cordy tips her face to the sky and flakes of snow whirl around us in the middle of the empty street. "I have feelings for you, Mark. Big ones. Big fat annoyed feelings. Don't talk to me about feelings. They're useless."

If what she explained is true, she has not one, but two men who think she's great, and she's refusing to see the worth in herself. Enough. Without thought, I swipe a leg under her, and she slips on the ice, landing hard. "Ow! Geez Louise, Mark!"

Crap. Sometimes I forget we're not twelve anymore. "I'm sorry. I shouldn't have done that. I forgot we were on ice instead of snow. " As if that explains my childish physical impulses. My phone buzzes in my pocket, and I ignore it. "Are you okay?"

"Just be grateful you have Lisa on your back, or you'd be next."

"Fair enough." With my hand on the elbow of her

plum-colored coat, I help her rise and brush the snow from her back.

"Why did you do that? That was mean."

The snow clings to escaped curls from her hat, and I watch the tiny flakes melt and disappear on her freckled nose. "I'm—I think I'm jealous." Wow. Maybe I am... I've got barely a year to find a wife. Cordy already has two men circling, and she's not even trying. She flips up a messy bun and can't keep men away. It could be so easy if she'd embrace what's right in front of her.

"Of me?"

I nod. Not that I want to take away what she has, but here I've spent two hours of my morning planning how to obtain what has fallen naturally, organically right into Cordy's path.

I keep a grip on her coat as we pick our way over the ice onto a less slippery area of the road and remind myself there's nothing wrong with the way I'm going about it. Introductions from friends and relatives, purposeful dates where we both know what we're looking for. I've written a clear outline for the kind of wife that matches my ideals and vision. My way leaves less to chance. Which is better. I shake off my momentary doubt that there's anybody out there for me.

Cordy seems to zip in and out of countless relationships that haven't gone anywhere. I chose my next words carefully. "I've seen you struggle. I've seen you try so hard through the years to please everyone, and try to fit yourself into someone's idea of what you should be. Someone you're not. You'll never be loved for who you are if you're trying to be someone else."

When I meet Future-Wife, I don't want to build any kind of front. And I don't want her to either. If we can't be honest and real with each other, it's not for me. I think about adding those details to my list, but no, I don't need to. It's a clear standard in my life already. Be kind, but always be honest. That shouldn't be so hard. If I can't be honest for fear of hurting someone's feelings, a marriage would never work between us.

I take in a deep breath and hold the door open for the crew right as my phone vibrates again.

It's Emily, my assistant in Phoenix. Emily never calls on Saturdays. Not unless something's on fire. And nothing is ever on fire in my office.

3

———

MARK

"What is it?" I answer Emily's call.

"Mark, you're never going to believe this." She sounds on the verge of panic. Her low voice carries an edge of desperation through the phone pressed tightly to my ear as I try to listen to her against the chaos surrounding me.

"Mrs. Emmerson offered the promotion to Randy," I say with a nonchalance I don't feel.

This isn't a good morning check-in the Saturday before Christmas. I didn't expect it to be, but part of me still hoped it was something trivial. Our adventurous blizzard walk of two blocks has me sweating through my borrowed coveralls. Over the heads of four excited kids—and one squirrely Aunt Cordy—I survey the almost empty trays of donuts. Lauren is trying to explain something to me, and Landon steps on my foot. A full Nebraska snowstorm blocks the view from the windows. The toddler harness is the last straw, ushering in the familiar edge of claustrophobia. I'm trapped. Even though I know I'm not. Too many things vie for my attention at once.

I've got to get Emily off the phone.

"How did you know?" She breathes out the confirmation. "Mrs. Emmerson offered the promotion to Randy. What are we going to do? Are you mad? You should be mad. I'm mad. That job is yours."

"It's still mine."

Lisa kicks her legs against my back and releases a shriek into my other ear. I grab one of her purple boots and hold it against my side.

This promotion will still be mine. I reassure Emily, "Don't worry about Randy."

"Why should I not be worried?" She puffs out air. She's frazzled, and it's annoying. We're a good team because she's the most level-headed, no-nonsense assistant at Lakeview Publishing. I hired her specifically because she knows how to get things done efficiently without a bunch of chatter. Right now, she's unraveling and I don't have the bandwidth to deal with it. Calling me on a Saturday morning? As if there's anything we can do about this news this weekend. She should know better than this.

"Randy won't accept it. He can't. He's settled firmly in Phoenix with a wife, two kids, and in-laws. A golden retriever. He's chained. A promotion won't do him any good if he has to relocate to New York."

Emily continues, an unattractive whine entering her voice, "We had it planned, Mark. *You* were getting the promotion. It was going to be my triumph of the year. The best assistant in the history of assistants gets her boss promoted. The end. That was our story."

"Thank you. I'm still going to New York." Heat burns around my neck. I rip off my sock cap and unzip the coveralls before I completely overheat. Now that I'm in line for donuts, and no longer forging through the blizzard, this getup is stifling. My gloved fingers claw the buckle of the harness of Lisa's imprisonment—and mine. Phone to my ear in one hand, I bite the end of my glove to get this straitjacket loosened.

Emily continues to prattle. I cut her off without waiting for her to finish. "We'll deal with it this afternoon. Send me what you know, and I'll touch base with you at one o'clock today." I pause my fumbling to think clearly. No, can't at one. Promised the kids sledding. It's a whole day of adventures with Uncle Mark. Quickly clicking through and dismissing other options for today, I realize my mistake was answering the phone to begin with. The only reason I have it on me is to contact Diana if needed. I wasn't about to take five kids without a life-line. "Emily, today doesn't work for me. You have my schedule. I'm blocked this whole weekend. Please don't call me again."

Around the mayhem of Cordy attempting to wrangle the five-year-olds, I barely hear Emily's intake of breath. "You're right, um, sorry. Thought you'd want to know. Okay, bye. Merry Christmas."

"Mark!" Cordy tugs at my sleeve. "Pay attention, do you want the regular glazed or the bear claw?"

My gaze follows her pointed mitten toward the few pastries left on the shelves. "What's a bear claw?" I raise my eyebrows.

"Who's going to New York? Why are you on the phone? It's donut time." Cordy doesn't realize she's putting on a dance show for the customers sitting in the booths along the wall. Fists together in front of her she's doing the shopping-cart-march-in-place... oh, step-to-the-left... step-to-the-right. It's not really her fault. The music drifting from the dust-covered speakers on the ceiling has taken over her brain cells.

I put my hands on her waist, move her behind me, and make eye-contact with the silver-haired man in an apron behind the cash register. After a deep, calming sigh, I smile. "Good morning."

He smiles and nods but doesn't open his mouth.

"We're almost too late, I see."

The man, Earl, according to his name tag, nods again. The racks behind him hold a half tray of donut holes, a bear claw—whatever that is—two twists, and a spattering of sprinkled options. There's nobody in line behind us. I hesitate a moment—I really hate to be *that guy*, but we've got a lot of people to feed here. "We'll take everything."

That's when I notice the hand-written *Cash Only* note stuck to the register with yellowed tape. Of course. I rock on the heels of my boots. "Cordy." The serious tone of my voice puts the kibosh on her dance. She sidles up beside me with Leo—or Lance—sitting on her foot. "I don't have cash," I whisper.

"Crap!" She pulls a face that exposes her bottom teeth then sticks out her tongue. Then she crosses her eyes.

"That's not helpful." I poke her nose. "Is there an ATM nearby?"

A woman rises from the nearest booth wearing neon pink scrubs with a yellow thermal undershirt. "I've got it," she says with a bright smile. Blond hair spills from a tangled blob on top of her head and leftover makeup smudges around blue eyes. She's about my height and fills out the top of her scrubs. Bright pink nails that match her outfit refocus my gaze as she slides a bill along the counter toward Earl, who's finished dumping the tray of donut holes into a paper bag.

Mariah Carey and her "Oooh, Baby" fades from the speakers as I politely intercept this ruffled blond woman and her offering. Before Earl notices the bill, I try to give it back to her while he fills another box. "Thanks for the offer, but that's not necessary."

She folds her arms over her chest with hands tucked to her sides. "Too bad, Mister. I'm not taking it back." Her lips quirk to the side, hiding a smile.

Lauren and Landon have both made their way behind the counter with Earl. Is that allowed? "Please just point me to the nearest ATM." I glance behind for Cordy, and she's got her hands full with the twins. With another twist that expels a laugh from Lisa on my back, I face Pink Scrubs and catch her with hands pulling out her ears in a monkey face.

"That was for Lisa." She purses her lips in what looks like an attempt to keep a straight face, then dissolves into laughter. "I don't toss out the monkey face for everyone." She clears her expression at my raised eyebrows then nods to the door. "Come on. There's an ATM right outside."

I worry about her lack of coat as she exits the shop before me. "Hey, I'm sure I can find it. Get back in there before you freeze to death."

"What? In this?" Her hands gesture to the low, white sky, palms toward the blizzard swirling around her like an enchantress. "Yer not from around these parts, are ya?" she says in a western drawl.

"I grew up near here, actually."

She waves a dismissive hand as snowflakes fill the air between us. "Oh, poor sucker."

"What?"

"Not you. Chris." She brackets her face and yells to a

teenager wearing shorts, snow boots, and a black hoodie making his way across the street. "Chris! It's no use. Earl's just sold out!"

Chris slumps his shoulders and does a complete turn-about without answering.

"Where's the ATM?"

"There's not one." She widens her eyes. "I'm a dirty liar. Take the money."

"Fine. What's your Venmo."

"Don't be like that, Mark." She scolds as if used to bickering with me.

"How'd you know my name?"

"How would I not know your name? You're the Phoenix runaway! I'm messing, let it go." She mock punches my shoulder at my confusion.

This woman is strange to say the least. I don't like that she knows things about me, and I know nothing about her. It puts me at a disadvantage when all I'm trying to do is pay for a few donuts. If that weren't enough, she's irritating with her inability to answer simple questions. I run my hand over my cold face.

"Hey, friend. Everything's fine. You're in Hadley Springs now. We know everything about everybody. It's no secret that Cousin Mark flew in from the Sunshine State. You're here with CJ, she's with Diana's kids. You've got Lisa on your back. Two and two is four not six."

"Florida is the Sunshine State."

"You trying to tell me Arizona isn't sunny? Look, Mark, I'm just saying that we know who you are. Welcome to town."

"I could have been any other visiting friend of the family." I clamp my mouth shut. Why am I feeding the ducks by arguing with her?

"I haven't heard of any other friends coming for the holidays." She tips her head, thinking. "Are there other friends coming this year? And I've never seen you before in my life because I was out of town last time you came."

"You're starting to get creepy."

She clicks her tongue. "Shucks, it's a shame, that. Let me buy donuts for my best friend's kids and move on with it."

"I don't like owing people. It makes me uncomfortable."

"Aren't you a straight shooter. I like that in men. Alright. I'll swap ya. Come with me to this hospital benefit fundraiser gala thing I must attend tonight, and we're square."

"Tonight?"

"Tonight. What are you deaf and stubborn?" She attempts to tuck in a few flyaways with her updo thing, and it's a complete waste of her efforts.

"I'm not—"

"That was out of line. Excuse me. It's been a long day."

"It's not even eight in the morning."

"Gosh, is it that late already? No wonder. I got to get some sleep. Then I have this fancy gown to put on. I should probably wash my hair. I look terrible. Whew. Lots to do." Her keys jingle as she talks with her hands. "Be ready by five. If you didn't pack anything fancy, no worries. And let's be honest, why would you? We don't dress for dinner around here. Hah! John already has the tux ready to go. My brother, John. He was taking me tonight so I didn't have to go alone and sit with Dr. Kendrick. We would look amazing with you in tux. Gah, what a relief. I am so glad I ran into you. That's settled then. You keep the money. I'll send the tux over in a bit."

The door of the donut shop opens and rams my shoulder. I step away, grateful it missed Lisa. "Mark," Cordy says with her hand outstretched. "You get cash? We're ready to go."

I blink, trying to process. My brain is stuffed with the white flurries that cloud my vision. Cordy snatches the bill still in my glove, and then I'm attacked by the bear cubs, Lance and Leo.

Pink Scrubs Girl is gone. I frantically turn a circle, searching the waves of snow clouds. She didn't even have a coat. How did—where did—? I spy a flash of pink before she ducks into a red car across the street. A second later the lights flash and her Honda crawls past.

The window rolls down, and she waves. "Thanks so much! Be ready by five! See ya!"

*Roped.* An imaginary red pen strikes the words and more materialize faster than I can edit them.

*Hoodwinked.* Strike.

*Signed up like a prize pig at the county fair.* Strike.

"What just happened?" I mutter. While zipping the coveralls to my chin, I pull one of the twins off of the other as they block the door. "That's a dumb place to play. You'll get hit by the door. Go fight over there." I toss the kid into a fresh square of snow beside the door. Maybe there's a patch of grass underneath.

*Hornswoggled.* Strike.

The others file out of the shop, a large box with Lauren, and Cordy has the paper bag hanging from her teeth while she adjusts her mittens. Landon sees his younger brothers flopping around and takes a running leap, pro-wrestling style, and lands on top of them both.

"Diana has tomorrow pretty well organized, I think." Cordy walks away from the door, and I dumbly follow. "We've got church at nine, lunch back at her place, and our moms will swoop in sometime after breakfast on Christmas Day." She turns and skips sideways like an elementary P.E. class. "Have any ideas for tomorrow night? Christmas Eve? I forgot to ask if Diana's doing any special Christmas Eve things for the kids." Once we walk around the side of the shop, the wind attacks, and for the next few minutes there's no more talking as we duck our heads and push forward.

*Bamboozled.* Strike.

Lisa pushes into my back to fight against her confinement. I understand the feeling and walk faster, outpacing Cordy and Lauren, but find no relief for the confusion swirling in my brain. That woman is exactly what I don't need.

A blizzard walk sounded like a fun idea half an hour ago. Between the cold whipping my face and the sweat soaking my back, I'm having trouble remembering why I suggested this. Warring thoughts ready their catapults. How and why was Randy offered my promotion? Am I going on a date wearing a borrowed tuxedo?

*Ambushed.* Strike. I didn't agree to it.

She can't be serious. It doesn't make sense.

I adjust the hat around my ears and tighten my scarf. It's twenty-seven degrees and tolerable, aside from the wind. The boys are having a blast. The three of them are actually crawling a dozen feet ahead. One of them leaps with a yell and pretends to have trouble running against the wind, arms flailing like a kite tail until he's shot with an invisible laser gun. "Pew, pew, pew!" He throws himself into a snow drift.

That's right. I took them on this walk because we will have no peace the remainder of the day if we don't get them outside. No peace... She's dropping off a tux borrowed from someone named John. I don't even know her name! One last word pops in my mind and refuses to be deleted.

*Captured.*

She is chaos and trickery, two things I don't stand for. But I did. I stood right there, mute and flummoxed. I didn't sign anything. I didn't even nod my head, and yet why do I feel there's an RSVP with my name on it?

4

# NICKIE



My elation remains silent until the car window seals away the cold. From the side mirror, I see the kids and CJ join Mark outside the shop before the snow absorbs him. I manage to drive around the block before a gleeful squeal explodes. "Yes! Yes, yes, yes, *yes*. Thank you, God above. Mmm-*mmm*. Hallelujah. Amen."

The moment I find an opening in the snow piles beside the road, I pull over, slam it into park, and yank out my phone. The text from Preston Kendrick still sears the home screen, unanswered from mere minutes ago. I sat in that donut booth scarfing down a plate of eggs, thinking of my warm bed and how I couldn't wait to reunite with it, when the anxiety-inducing text buzzed into my life.

> Dr. Kendrick: Too bad about Hadley Strings missing their audition. Since John is still stuck in Omaha, no reason for us not to go together. I'll swing by and you can ride with me tonight.

Call me for an emergency C-Section after a thirty-hour labor any day over dealing with Preston. But managing both in the same day is asking a bit much of my nervous system. I breathe out another sigh of praise to God as I form a response to my colleague.

> Nickie: Yeah, John's pretty bummed, but he'll bounce back. If it's meant to be, they'll get another chance. And thanks for the offer, you're too kind! But, as it happens, sorry, I've got a date for tonight. I appreciate you thinking of me.

Ew, gag. Go away. Leave me alone.

I mutter a response that I would never in all my life say out loud. "I don't like to be around you, Dr. Preston Kendrick. I hate it when you make assumptions about me. I've made it pretty clear over the years that I don't want to be your date or girlfriend."

His reply is immediate.

> Dr. Kendrick: Really? I assumed you were dragging John with you again this year.

Dragging John? Harsh. I never drag John anywhere. My brother is insanely supportive and has never once complained about attending this yearly event. He pretends to be fancy in his fancy suit and distributes business cards for his fancy band, Hadley Strings. Why would I drag him? I want to say many, *many* things, but I keep it short.

> Nickie: I've got a date.

> Dr. Kendrick: Anyone I know?

My thumbs freeze while my mouth runs in the privacy of my car. "I don't have to tell you anything! I don't have to justify nothin'. I'm a grown-up woman who can refuse you with no excuses." I bolster my courage to ignore his question and even go so far as to delete the text thread. Take that!

Disappointment plops in my lap at an incoming text with his name.

> Dr. Kendrick: You're not manufacturing a mystery man are you? Just let me take you out. I promise you won't regret it. Give us a shot.

I blow steam from my nose. On the inside I'm Donald Duck kicking and pacing and Ra-ra-ra-ra-RA! And nobody pays me any mind. My thumbs punch with unnecessary force while I preach my response.

"Preston, I find your candor *quite* insulting. You've pushed beyond the boundaries of professionalism when I have done everything to courteously avoid a relationship! We've worked together for many years and although I'll be the first to acknowledge that you're a wonderful doctor, I have zero interest in forming a relationship with you outside of work. I haven't been home in thirty-six hours and my patience is non-existent, which I think you are well aware of and trying to push me into accepting. Leave. Me. Alone."

I type it. And then delete, delete, delete, delete... and try again.

> Nickie: Thank you for your offer, but I have a date for the evening.

Good enough.

I toss the irritating device onto the cupholder and jam the gear into drive. When I turn the wheel to pull into the street a flash of blue in my periphery startles me, and I slam the brake.

A large truck ambles past, hopefully unaware that I almost pulled in front of it. My heart is in my throat, and I feel a thousand times the fool. Visibility is low through the curtains of falling snow, even though the snowstorm has lessened considerably since this morning. But that's no excuse for what I almost did.

Carefully checking all mirrors this time, I slowly ease into the middle of the road with shaking hands. I imagine a blaring horn the moment before impact and the crunch of metal and breaking glass.

"I'm good," I whisper encouragement. "I'm good!" But I'm not listening to the comforting words and bite an exasperated sigh. "Nickie Brader, you are too smart for this. Get yourself home and to bed. You cannot let your guard down like that."

I would've advised anyone else not to drive themselves home after the insane shift I completed. But the refreshing snow on my face energized me enough to ignore the fatigue. I'm fine. I'll be home in a minute.

Let's think of happier things. Happier things like the gala tonight. What a fortuitous morning this has been! Good things are always happening to me. Let's think about those chocolate brown eyes of Diana's cousin. His drop-dead gorgeousness with Lisa on his back like some kind of he-man babysitter. Diana never mentioned that about him. He's wonderful with the kids. He's only in town for a few days so we get to have fun without any commitment from either of us. Ta-da! Perfection.

How lucky am I that he appeared in my line of sight the moment after Preston's text? I was sinking into despair, I had no idea how to politely get out of a night of his company, and then *Hello, stranger from out of town with a face that steals the hearts of women of every age.*

His calmness with the kids around him, and his playfulness with CJ, caught my attention once I tore my gaze away from his face. I knew the moment he noticed the Cash Only sign and burst from my seat, swallowing the last bite of eggs. *I'll save you!*

I hadn't even thought to haul him to the gala until he refused the money. Then it all fell into place like fate! Not fate. Divine intervention. The angels are working in my favor.

I chuckle when I remember his stammering reply when I efficiently rescheduled his entire evening. He didn't stand a chance of refusal because I didn't leave room for—

I gasp. And it's forceful enough to throw me into a coughing fit.

Heaven, help me. What have I done? Did I just *Preston Kendrick* this poor man at the donut shop? Oh. My. Lanta. I didn't even give him a *chance* to say no. I was so desperate to escape my own predicament I didn't even look before pouncing on the first unassuming gentleman. Doesn't matter how perfect his physique. That probably makes this whole thing even worse!

Rotten doesn't begin to describe what I'm feeling. And I've already spouted off to Preston that I have a date. If I let Mark off the hook, which I absolutely must, I really will have to go alone. Then Preston will know that I'm full of stupid excuses, and he'll gloat and try to impress me throughout the whole stupid evening. I could play sick! I could not go at all and wait for tomorrow.

"Tooomorrow! I love ya! Tomorrow! You're only a day away."

No. Orphan Annie's not helping because I'm in a mess that I can't actually hide from. Tomorrow doesn't erase today, and it won't erase tonight. Tomorrow will arrive, and

I can't go into it lying about being sick when I wasn't. Especially when I'm in charge of the welcome speech to kick off the evening. I kinda have to be there. Nothing for it but to call Diana and cancel with Mark.

So much for dreams coming true for this Cinderella. That girl had a fairy godmother after all who explained all the rules. I have…

I bark a laugh. Okay, I have an all-powerful Creator, which is much better. "Yep." I tap my palm against the hood of the car. "Sorry. I thought Mark was a rescue gift from You. But I didn't handle that very well, did I? I'm like a shark waiting for dinner. Good golly. So, hey… I didn't want to lie to Preston about having a date. I don't suppose You'd send in reinforcements? I need to go to this thing tonight. I don't want to go with Preston. He's being weird about it. I don't want to be a liar about having a date when I don't have one. Uggghhh. God, can you, um, fix this for me?"

I hate disappointing people. If I didn't have a reputation to uphold, I'd be tempted to go to bed and accidentally-on-purpose not set an alarm. But nobody would believe that to be possible for me. It would never work. And either way, I'd still have to contact Mark.

For the sake of my conscience, I have to do something about this before I sleep.

I park on the snow-covered driveway in front of the craftsman-style house I share with my grandparents. The weight of the phone in my hands threatens to undo me. How in the world can I cancel with Mark and not have lied to Preston?

With a plea for guidance, I make a call to Diana. "Please answer… or don't answer. Maybe don't answer. Tell me I didn't ruin Christmas with donuts."

5

# MARK



After we clear the table from breakfast—which lasted mere seconds before disappearing into the children—the three boys drag Cordy down the hall, Lisa follows, Lauren flops on the floor in front of the couch, and Diana with Jack on her hip lowers herself to the chair beside me with an unconscious sigh. "Okay, Mark. What happened this morning? Explain. Are you feeling okay? Need to go back to bed?"

Diana's the older sister I never had and will see through anything I try to shrug off. Maybe if I pretend hard enough Pink Scrubs Girl will disappear from my memories like a bad dream. A lot happened this morning, but Diana doesn't need to trouble herself.

"I'm—Yeah, my assistant called. There's an opening for a promotion we've been working toward, and there seems to have been a mix-up." I drag my knuckles side to side on the table. "I'm the best candidate, but they've offered it to someone else."

"What're you going to do? Can you get to the bottom of it today? You're not one to sit around and let things happen to you."

"Nah, it's Saturday. Tomorrow's Christmas Eve, then Mom's coming up. It'll hold until I get home."

Jack tries to stick his hand in her mouth, and she bats his hand away unfazed. "Well, if you're sure. But you look a little... slumpy."

"Yeah, maybe a nap would be good." Before the blizzard walk, I was giving Cordy a hard time about this Gilbert she's been texting non-stop. My cousins would freak out if they heard about what happened to me today. That woman was obviously not stable.

The more I analyze it, the more that explains it. She wasn't dressed in scrubs because she's a nurse or something. She probably requires care for herself! She's an escaped patient who ran off to the donut shop because she hates hospital food.

Obviously... because... I shake the thoughts away with a jerk of my head. She was driving. And she knew who I was...

I drop my head in my hands and sigh.

"Oh, buddy." Diana rubs her hand on my back like a mother. "Why don't you go lie down for a while."

A text comes through Diana's phone, and she removes her hand. A second later she emits a high-pitched squeal that startles Jack, so he cries. "Mark!"

"What?" I lurch to my feet, ready to protect her from a bear.

"Nickie's taking you to the gala tonight." Her face is aglow, and she releases a giggle. I have not heard Diana giggle in... ever. "Here." She pushes Jack against my chest and lifts the phone to her ear.

"Yes. He's right here... No, he didn't say anything to me about it... Oh, do you think so?" She laughs while looking at me. "You're probably right... No, no. I think it's a great idea... Absolutely. No! Don't say such things. Of course he wants to go with you... I'll ask him."

I sit back down, hard. "I don't want to go."

Diana touches her finger to my top lip. "Mark says he wants to go... Probably he was too flabbergasted to mention it... Mmm-hmm... Yes. He wants to go... No, you didn't twist his arm... Oh, sure, that'll be fine... Nickie, baby, calm down. You are not Preston! Yes, Mark is going with you, and he's going to love it. Who wouldn't want to go with you? If I didn't have Jack I'd make you take me instead... Yep... Yep... I think eleven. Hang on." Diana angles the phone away from her mouth. "What size shoe do you wear?"

"Tell her I'm not going. I don't want to go."

She rolls her eyes and scuttles to the back entry. After digging through our mountainous wet pile of snow boots, she finds the tennis shoes I wore on the flight yesterday. "Eleven... Yes! He says he's excited about it."

"No." I rise from the table, clutching the baby to my chest, and Diana hops away and runs from the kitchen. Jack laughs to see his mom playing, as if it's a big game. I don't chase her because I'm not playing. Jack squirms, and I hold him away from my body facing me. "Whhhyyyy?" I gently shake him at arm's length, just enough to jiggle his fat cheeks. "Quit laughin', kid. Uncle Mark is under attack. You're supposed to be on my team."

I growl with my deepest, scariest voice. Jack's expression turns serious for a second and then he opens his mouth to show off a row of new teeth, and a string of drool falls to the floor.

"That's gross." After I wipe his face with the hand towel

on the counter, I sling him under one arm and bring him to Lauren in the next room. She's curled into a ball on the floor next to the couch. "What are you doing?"

"Warm," she mumbles.

I step closer and hot air wafting from under the couch sends a wave of comfort over my socked feet. "Oh, you're right." I sit beside her on the floor. "Warm."

Jack flops out of my arms and crawls over his sister until he's practically sitting on her head. She shoves him off, and he loses the small bit of balance he'd mastered and rolls backward like a baby panda bear. He's squishy and floppy and now he's mad and lets out a shriek as he crawls back to Lauren's head.

"Stop it, Jack," says Lauren when he smooshes his hands on her face and drool puddles on her forehead. "Ugh, Jack!" She shoves him, and when he falls he lays still like a wounded thing. His bottom lip protrudes and real tears appear the moment before he lets out a wail.

Diana enters, tucking her phone in the pocket of her sweatpants, and pauses by the end of the couch. "Mark, I thought you were watching him."

"I was. I am. He brought this on himself." I wave my hand toward the guilty party. "He's fine. Dude's gotta learn he can't sit on people's heads." On cue, Jack's wail turns into a scream, and he kicks his legs repeatedly against Lauren's face.

"Uh-uh," I admonish and turn the baby so he can have his tantrum without hurting anyone. "See?" I show Diana it's not my fault. "He started it."

Diana sighs. "Lauren, get up. You can't let him bully you like that. It's time for his nap anyway. Did you finish your math yet?"

Lauren was halfway into a sitting position, but at the

mention of math, she loses all bone structure and melts to the carpet. She doesn't scream but performs a ten-year-old version of Jack's tantrum with her fists pummeling the carpet.

I link my fingers together in my lap and smile at Diana. "So... kids are fun..."

Diana accuses me with a glare as if I've caused this double display.

"Don't look at me. I'm just visiting. These are your spawn."

Lauren shoots her head up. "Spawn?" She bares her teeth. "Really? Spawn?"

Diana chuckles as she lifts Jack from the floor, who immediately quiets and snuggles into her. "Math, Lauren. Finish it now or no Christmas for you."

As Diana walks away, I call after her. "I hope you told her I'm not going."

"You're going." She doesn't even have the decency to look at me.

What happened to free will? What happened to autonomy and adulthood? R-E-S-P-E-C-T. Shouldn't I have a say in whether or not I go to a black-tie event with a crazy chick in pink pajamas? I haven't agreed to anything and nobody's going to make me go if I don't want to go. When I go out it's because I want to. And I never want to hang out with people who rip the floor out from under me and then laugh when I fall. This girl has trouble written all over her. If she were a manuscript, I'd toss her back in the slush pile. She's a Did Not Finish.

Lauren and I sit side by side and watch Diana take the baby down the hallway. My fingers itch to dig my notebook out of my backpack and either damage control whatever Emily was freaking out about this morning or add notes to my new mission, *Project: Find a Wife*. I need to do something. Sitting in limbo, waiting around, has already begun to make me anxious.

I know I can't start on either until I return to Phoenix. My friends there have their own holidays to attend, and I won't bother them until after the first of the year. But I could write out the list of who I need to contact. Plan a few date itineraries. Research restaurants, activities for couples. I haven't been on a serious date since moving to Phoenix, so I don't know the first place to start.

Inviting a date back to my place isn't an option since I live in a hotel. I doubt a respectable woman would appreciate that. Though, there is the pool and the gym... No. I wonder if I'd find a woman willing to live in a hotel? Once kids come along it's not ideal. But for two working adults, why not take advantage of a hot breakfast, no upkeep, and a cleaning service? I'm baffled that more people don't live this way.

If I could get at least two introductions to possible candidates from a few trusted friends in Arizona... It wouldn't take but a handful to start the project. Thinking positively, perhaps I'd even meet someone on the first month of dates. Things could go really well.

But that's for later. Tomorrow morning I'll get the chance to look through it again during my blocked-out power hour of work. I'm wearing the fun Uncle Mark hat today. The wife project will hold.

I glance at my little blond cousin beside me. Her hair is mussed from Jack's extra love. She's wearing an oversized red sweatshirt stained with speckles of yellow paint on one sleeve, black leggings with a hole in the knee, and fluffy pink socks.

"Math is stupid," Lauren grumbles to the ceiling.

"I thought if you were homeschooled you didn't have to do school over the holidays."

"Not if your mom makes you do all the problems. If you're homeschooled you have to do math every day forever until you diiieee..." Head still resting on the cushion, she rolls her face to look at me, begging me to commiserate with her.

"That sounds awesome! You're the luckiest girl in the world. You get to do math forever!"

"Shut up, stupid."

"Ooo. Good one." I punch the side of her leg.

"Ow!" Lauren tries to grab my hand, but I evade her and punch her other leg. *Bop, bop, bop.* I pummel until she stops trying to catch my fists and instead palms me in the face. That catches me by surprise, and I laugh.

"Okay, enough." I grab her wrist and force her to punch herself in the cheek. "Get the math out. I'll help you, okay? Let's go. We have a full schedule this afternoon."

"When are you going out with Nickie?"

"Who's Nickie?"

"Duh, the one mom was talking to on the phone."

"I'm not going anywhere with that woman." I drop her hands and sit back.

"Yeah, you are. I heard Mom before you came in. You're so lucky. Nickie is the funniest. Can I do your hair? I'm really good at doing hair. You don't want to go like it is now, 'cause you look like a monkey-bear."

"You look like a visiting she-goose from Jupiter."

"That's not even a real thing."

"Neither is a monkey-bear. Get your math."

"No." Lauren digs her shoulder into my side and tries to push me over.

"Yes." I push back by simply not moving.

We have a silent fight about it, and I'm sure the poor girl is trying, but all I have to do is lean over. "Bwahahaha," I taunt in my Bowser voice as my niece is smooshed against the carpet beneath my back.

"Ughhh, fine." Her words are muffled against the floor.

I spread my arms and bask in the warm air pouring from the vent somewhere beneath the couch. Lauren huffs in her struggle to get away. "Also," I inform her, "I'm not going out with Nickie."

She wriggles herself free. "Yes, you are."

"No."

"Yes."

"Why?"

Lauren rolls her eyes. "Because you're not really that stupid."

6

———

## NICKIE

Once I'm off the phone with Diana, a wave of exhaustion accompanies the relief. Mark is still on for tonight. Picking my way through the ten inches of snow on the drive, I think about how I'm going to get this cleared, feed the grandparents, sleep, and fix my hair. I could survive with only a three-hour nap, but my body is craving a full shift of sleep before I clock in again.

I smile at the snow covering my boots with each step, happy that the sidewalk hasn't been shoveled since before I left for work yesterday. I was worried all morning Grandpa would try to move the snow by himself.

"I'm home!" I holler into the living room and meet Grandpa zipping his coat. "What are you doing?"

"I'm going out to shovel."

"That sounds like too much excitement for today."

"Excitement? Why, I got nothin' to do 'round here but watch the weather!" He speaks in his best Calamity Jane accent.

"Whip-crack-away, Grandpa, but the answer's still no. I love that you're willing to do John's chores, but I'll handle it in a few minutes. I need to get the tux out of his room 'cause I caught a fresh date for the fundraiser tonight."

"You caught what, honey?" Grandma pushes her walker in from the kitchen. "Who did you get this time? And where is that boy?"

"John and Gilbert are stuck in Omaha until the interstate reopens. They'll probably be home tomorrow." I breeze into the living room and grab the blood pressure cuff from the coffee table.

Grandma pauses before her recliner that's sitting in its tilted ready-to-sit position. "Jeffrey, what are you doing?"

"Nothing," I interject before he defends himself. "He's coming for a ride with me to deliver the suit." That should wear him out enough to keep him from trouble while I sleep today.

"I'm allowed to move snow." He grumbles.

"You're not." I level him with my best glare. "Doctor's orders. But you can come for a ride. Just wait, don't... I'll be right back." Deciding to forego checking Grandma's vitals, I toss the cuff in its basket.

With the fear of Grandpa taking another fall spurring me to action, I dash up the stairs, taking two at a time, hoping everything is stored properly since John's last ritzy piano performance. In his closet, I locate the jacket, trousers, pleated shirt, satin bow tie, waistcoat, suspenders, pocket square, and polished patent leather shoes—whoops, almost forgot the cufflinks. John wears a size twelve shoe, but it'll have to be close enough. I hesitate over the top hat on the shelf and decide against it. That's probably a bit much for this event. Hoping I have it all, I sprint back before Grandma's even settled in her recliner.

Grandpa has managed to put on both of his boots by the time I'm ready at the door, able to help him to the car. "We'll be right back, Grandma!"

"It's a fine day for a blizzard." Grandpa holds his gloved hand open to catch tiny flakes of white crystals. "You won't need to go to the gala tonight. They'll cancel."

I grab the shovel and clear a single-wide path in front of Grandpa. "It's a big deal. The hospital counts on this night every year for a huge chunk of their donations. They can't cancel."

He raps me on the hip with his cane. "The interstate is closed."

"It is, but we have farmers and their tractors clearing the local roads around here. We don't need the interstate."

"They will reschedule for the day after Christmas."

"How do you know so much?" I chuck the shovel toward the porch and open the passenger door for him.

He doesn't answer and soon we're cruising through the empty, white streets of Hadley Springs.

"I met a guy."

Grandpa grunts, then hums in thought until we turn another corner. "Who are his parents? They from around here?"

"I don't know. He's Diana's cousin, Mark. And let me tell you, Grandpa. He is *fine*. He had Lisa on his back in a harness, she's the one with the curly hair that tries to run off with your cane every Sunday. Mark was wrangling all of Diana's kids like a professional. Then when he didn't have cash, cause you know Earl only takes cash still—"

"Good for him. You can't trust those machines. If the power goes out, the whole world shuts down."

"But not Earl. We'll still be able to buy donuts. In the dark, with no heat. You're ridiculous. If the power goes out, the card machines will be the least of our worries." I think of the multiple generators, the back-up, and extra back-up systems we have at the hospital to make sure we aren't ever in that situation. But hey, sure. Cash-only donuts.

Grandpa hums then says, "So you saved his donuts."

"I did! I exactly did." We arrive outside Diana's house, and I press the hazards. "In return for my rescuing, he's taking me to the gala in place of John who's stuck in Omaha."

"He offered."

"Ehhh." My head rocks from side to side. "I didn't provide him a way out, but he's game."

"And then you'll rewrite his entire future when he falls at your feet."

I flash a smile at my sweet Grandpa. "Bless his beautiful hide."

"Does he quote musicals?"

"Not yet." I widen my eyes and dance my eyebrows.

Grandpa laughs with me and drops into his Calamity Jane accent again. "I got a strange feelin' somebody's bein' hustled."

"Nah, you know I'm messing around. I don't need no stinkin' man to take care of me." I unbuckle and contort myself over the seat to grab the tux. I grunt at the awkward position as I admit aloud, "Though I sure don't mind looking."

"Shame on you."

I sit back down with the garment bag over my lap. "Granted, I did manipulate him into the date. Diana assures me he's happy to go with me. But we'll just see what we see. He lives in Arizona. So it's not like it'll ever work anyway. Whew!"

"Arizona's not so far." Grandpa moves like he's going to get out of the car.

"Stay here. I'm going to run in and drop this off." I stop and let out a laugh. "Arizona is far. It's about as far as you can get."

"Not as far as Guam."

"You're very right. Stay here."

"No, I'm going to meet him." He taps the hook of his cane against the window.

"You can't. You'll scare him off."

"If you caught him, girl, how would I scare him?"

"Fair, but I'm still asking you not to, because I've been awake all night and then some. I'm drunk on sleep-deprivation—I wouldn't pass any kind of test."

Grandpa's entire countenance changes, like a weight has been strapped to his shoulders. "Okay."

"You really wanted to go in, huh?" Working overnights for the ER at the hospital is the thing I hate most about this career. The job itself is fine, but I hate how I can't be truly available for my family. I missed years while in school. I'm determined to make up for it now.

Today, I've been away for too many hours, my grandparents need help with the house and themselves, yet claws of exhaustion now slice the edges of my brain. I've been off work for barely an hour. I always call ahead at Earl's for breakfast of scrambled eggs, hashbrowns, and fruit—most people don't even know he has a menu, and now I've yet to steam the dress for tonight, shovel the snow, feed the cats, make sure Grandma takes her meds...

"You need sleep, Dr. Brader." Grandpa says the words, but his eyes plead to let him go in and play. I took his driver's license away two years ago. That was one of the hardest decisions Mom and I had to make for him. Sometimes I wonder if he's yet to forgive me. Even though Mom is as involved as she can be, with her and Dad running the daycare from their home, we all felt the best arrangement was for John and me to move in with Grandpa and Grandma. I have the medical training to keep an eye on them, and John is usually around to do heavy lifting, especially since he and Gilbert built the sound booth upstairs. Mom or Dad can still check on them throughout the day, but Grandpa misses his independence.

Holding out an olive branch, I offer an alternative. "I could leave you here, go home to bed, then grab you later. I'll call Aunt Jewels to come sit with Grandma for a while."

Appeased, he nods. "You do that. I'll bring in the doo-duds."

"I'll bring in the doo-duds, you walk without falling on your face in the snow. And I need you to promise me you won't scare Mark. He seems like a level-headed guy, and we don't need him thinking weird things about us."

"I hold a no-scare guarantee."

"Whatever. I'll believe it when I see it. Come on, then."

An age and a half later, when we finally shuffle our way to the door, nobody answers our knock, so I let us inside. The sound of absolute mayhem answers from across the kitchen in the living room. A collection of animal noises is forefront, with the general commotion of clapping hands and yells and hoots.

"Enough!" Mark's command silences the children.

I help Grandpa take off his boots, and we make it inside.

Mark is wearing a royal blue satin cape that only hangs to his waist over a black T-shirt, sweatpants, and a plastic gold crown on his head. He's brandishing a dry-erase marker at one of the five-year-old twins, who's crawling toward him in a tiger suit. "Get back, fiend!"

Resting on the couch behind Mark is a large whiteboard with the unsolved equation of four hundred eighty-seven divided by six.

"Now, Lauren. See here. You've got hundreds of unicorns on your farm. Hey, sit up. They're beautiful. So beautiful you've started a unicorn rental business."

For fear of interrupting, I ease back before we're seen and quietly pull out a chair for Grandpa at the table. The lights are off here in the kitchen, and the others don't seem to be aware of us. I stand behind Grandpa to watch how this plays out.

Lauren clasps her hands together under her chin. "They could come to birthday parties!"

"Exactly, but think bigger. You've trained them to march in parades and do tricks. You rent them out in huge herds for massive events. You're running the largest unicorn rental operation in all of Nebraska."

One of the wrestling tigers shouts, "In all of 'Merica!"

The other echoes, "'Merica!"

Mark taps the number six on the white board. "But listen, you have six different events booked for tomorrow. Christmas Eve is a big day for the unicorn business. We need to sort them into their proper groups. And you need to be sure they're equal or the companies will get upset with you if they think you're being unfair. How are you going to sort them into groups?"

"Probably by color."

Mark laughs. "Sure, you can sort them by color, but they're all covered in snow right now and you can't tell which is which. So let's start sorting and see what happens. If there are four groups of a hundred unicorns each, how many is that?"

Lauren shrugs.

Mark looks back at Lauren and slowly fills his chest with a breath. He smiles gently then gestures to the white board. "If you're running your business with four hundred and eighty-seven unicorns and you have four hundred *here*." He circles the four over and over. "How many left in the field?"

Landon shouts, "Eighty-seven."

"Landon! Stop. It's my question!" But then Lauren covers her face with both hands and her shoulders shake. "I hate math, and I hate it, hate it, hate it."

Mark removes his plastic crown and scratches his head all around. He puts the crown on Lisa and unhooks his cape. "Boys, why don't you take Lisa to your room and see about that fort you were building?"

The two tigers roar and scamper down the hallway and Landon scoops up his toddler sister and follows. Mark slides to the floor and leans against the couch.

"Lauren, that's enough."

She raises her head with eyes filled with tears.

He grabs a tissue box from under the side table for her. "You're not allowed to cry over math."

"But I hate it, and I can't even do it."

Mark tosses the cape to the floor. "That's *enough*." His tone is firm, even a bit harsh. "You are not allowed to say you can't do it. You can hate it all you want, and that won't make it go away. You have a choice to keep working on it, ask for help, and keep at it until you figure it out. Or you can whine and cry and complain about how much you hate it. You choose that second one and you'll be whining and crying your whole life. You'll be the most miserable girl in the world because you decided you can't do something."

Her fists clench and press against her stomach "But I can't—"

"Stop." He's firm but doesn't raise his voice. "You may say, 'This is a challenge.' But don't you dare sit here and spout lies about *can't*."

I shift uneasily from my hideaway in the kitchen, tempted to intervene now. It was one thing to watch the kids play, but this is low-down spying. I move to step forward, but Grandpa raises his hand, a silent signal for us to stay put.

The girl sinks lower to the floor while her heels drum on the carpet, a bodily expression of emotions melting and raging at once. "But you don't get it, Mark. I really can't—"

"Ah! Stop!" Mark is a powerhouse of energy. He shoots to his knees and spreads his arms wide. "Am I talking to the wall? You're ten years old and you know how to read. Did you know how to read when you were five?"

"No." Lauren fidgets with a lock of her blond hair before letting it fall over her eyes.

"Because it was hard." Mark's a pacing Sunday preacher. "You hated it." A fist pounds into the palm of his other hand. "Five years ago, we were right here with you crying, *I can't*. Stop making me ride the same train, kid. I won't let you quit on yourself, because you can freaking do hard things."

The fire of his voice catches me off guard. He's not harsh, but the passion for his niece is undeniable.

Lauren sits straight with a gasp. "Mom says we're not allowed to say freaking."

Thumbs hooked on the band of his sweatpants, Mark blinks and draws in a slow breath. I recognize his subtle calming techniques before he points to the whiteboard on the couch. "Four hundred plus eighty-seven is how many?"

"Four hundred and eighty-seven, duh."

"Duh." Mark smirks. "So if you take away four hundred, how many are left?"

"Eighty-seven." She answers immediately.

"Thank you." He drops to the floor beside her again and gently brushes the hair away from her face, forcing her to really look at him. "Can you put four hundred unicorns into six groups of a hundred?"

She hesitates, and I've never wanted someone to get the right answer more in my life. We're rooting for you, kid!

"No," she answers slowly.

Mark's smile is all the praise she needs. He smiles, and Lauren lights up. I glance at Grandpa, and his eyes sparkle with happiness. He's nodding encouragement with his hands steepled over his lap.

"Only four. Which means to put them into six groups you will have *less than* one hundred in each group." Mark raps his knuckles on the coffee table shoved to the side of the room that's covered in coins. "Okay, back to where we started with the coins. You ready to work with these?"

When Lauren doesn't move, he loops his arms around her waist and physically relocates her in front of the coffee table. "Put the dimes back in their six piles. I think one of the tigers destroyed it."

She kneels in front of the table and slides the dimes into groups. "One, two, three..." Her voice pitches lower to a whisper. Lauren studies him, her expression questioning. "Is it eight? I get eight dimes in each group?"

Mark stretches onto the couch and throws an arm over his eyes. "Don't ask me as if you don't know. You counted forty-eight dimes into six groups. How many are in each group?"

"Ughh, I don't know! Just tell me if I got it right."

He doesn't move his arm from his eyes, but gestures

with his other hand. "Quit your fussing, She-Goose. You're not stupid. Tell me straight, with confidence."

"Eight?"

"Lauren."

"Eight."

"Alas, the people in charge don't care unless you write it on the board." He pulls himself from the couch and tosses her the dry-erase marker from his pocket. "Put the eight in the right place. I need more coffee. You need to hire a herd manager, stat, or your business is going bankrupt. How did you ever get six parties booked for the same weekend anyhow?"

I don't have a chance to move, think, or plan before Mark has turned our direction. He sees us—and I'm paralyzed. Caught and captured.

# 7

# NICKIE

NEWSIES SOUNDTRACK—HIGH TIMES, HARD TIMES

Mark makes eye contact from the living room. There's no sudden reaction as he walks toward me and Grandpa. Not even an eyebrow twitch.

Cool as a cucumber, he enters the kitchen and flips on the light. "My schedule is booked. I'm not going." He nods his head to the suit slung over my arm. "I don't need that."

"Won't matter," Grandpa answers. "They're going to postpone it for the day after Christmas."

Mark stops in front of Grandpa. While completely ignoring me, he juts out his hand. "Mark Brader. Nice to meet you."

His name is Brader? Really? How did Diana neglect to mention her cousin has the same last name as me?

Grandpa opens his mouth, shuts it, then smiles. "Jeffrey. Howdy do? I think you and Nick have things to discuss. I'll take over the unicorn farm if that's alright." With his hand still in Mark's he leans forward. "Help me up."

The tendons in Mark's forearm jump as he braces

himself against the table and offers his strength to Grandpa. Once Grandpa's up, Mark pushes in two chairs and kicks a stuffed shark out of Grandpa's path to the living room.

As a yawn squints my eyes, I lay the suit over the back of a chair and repeatedly pat my hand against my cheek. *Smack, smack, smack.* Wake up, wake up, wake up!

"All right." Mark stands in front of me. Short brown hair styled-yet-casual, black T-shirt simple-yet-quality, and his chin shows a thick shadow of stubble. Hands rest on low-riding sweatpants, shoulders straight and gaze serious. "Spill. What's going on here?"

The full image of him has momentarily stopped my tongue. How does a man in pajamas, or athletic-casual-wear, project an aura of immense authority? Hmm, I suppose it's no different than what I manage in scrubs half of the time.

His tanned arm gestures between me and himself. "Why have I been—" He spins his hand in the air, and I interrupt.

"Forced into a date?"

"I was going to say hoodwinked. Suckered."

"Bamboozled," I offer.

"No, I already struck that one." His pointer finger makes a little line through the air and mimes writing another word. "Drafted, maybe."

"Played?" I'd love to look away and hide my embarrassment, but his gaze hasn't left mine once. After a fortifying breath I force a gentle smile. I slap on my sharing-hard-news-with-a-patient emotional shield. "I am sorry, Mark. Diana assured me you were looking forward to this. I called her, you know, because I did feel bad about the way I handled things."

"Voluntold."

Oh. My. His expression hasn't softened this whole conversation! What does he want from me? "Wrangled?"

"Coffee?" He turns away, and I feel slighted by the easy dismissal.

"No thanks, I'm off to bed as soon as I get home. Though I need to check in with Diana about Grandpa. Jeffrey wants to hang here for the day. He's no trouble, but he should take a nap after lunch and don't let him try to fix anything."

With his back to me, Mark waits for the mug to fill. "So, what do you do? A night nurse or something?"

"Something. I'm a doctor."

He turns to me with eyebrows raised.

"What? You surprised?"

A smile graces his face. "I had you pegged wrong from the beginning." After a careful sip of his fresh refill he sets it on the counter with a heavy *clunk*. "I think what you did to me this morning was weird as all get out. You invited a stranger to attend a black-tie event. How does that make sense?" He crosses his arms and waits for my defense.

"You forget I'm best friends with Diana. You're not a stranger to me. You had her kids crawling all over you, and you were with CJ."

"Cordy."

"Cordy? Cordelia? She introduced herself as CJ."

He rolls his eyes. "Don't call her that. Cordy is fine. CJ doesn't exist."

"Regardless, I knew who you were." I shrug. "And you were worth any kind of risk over Dr. Kendrick thinking he can prance in—" My throat constricts a moment too late. How did I let myself blab that? Gossip is a sin. You'd think with all the secrets I keep, I'd know how to restrain my personal thoughts.

I'm not allowed to tell anyone that I delivered a baby last night via C-Section, that the current boyfriend was hungover and removed from the delivery room after he threw up, that the forty-year-old mother tested positive for drugs and the baby was immediately taken by social services. Or that Mrs. Crofter's cancer has returned and she's not telling her family. HIPAA violations are all the harder to avoid in this small town where everyone knows everything, yet I'm the one who knew it first and can't talk about it.

Then here I go spouting personal opinions about a certain doctor that cannot get back to him or anyone. We can't afford strained relationships with our work.

"He's a prancer, huh? Does he swagger a little when he walks?"

"I think he might, but I try to keep to my own business." A bubble of laughter builds at the thought, and I can't help but continue. "I'm not quite sure, would you mind demonstrating?"

Mark pushes away from the counter, strides to the corner of the kitchen, spins on the ball of his foot, and strikes a runway pose—duck lips included.

"Hmm," I let my gaze travel the length of his body. "No. That's not it."

"You're right. That was more of a strut." He laughs at himself as he walks back to retrieve his coffee. His head juts forward and back like a walking chicken. "Does he cavort?"

I whisper the word, thinking. "Prowl is closer."

Mark lowers his coffee, the teasing evaporates. "Hey, be serious. Are you safe with him?"

"Of course I'm safe. It's not like that. He's a respected professional. I— We—" How to explain myself without badmouthing? How can I say this delicately? I don't even like putting our names together in the same sentence. It'd be cool if I didn't have to explain anything and Mark would happily escort me, but he appears unconvinced.

I try again. "Preston Kendrick, although a wonderful doctor, has trouble understanding that I'm perfectly happy without a special man in my life. He's always trying to figure out how to be alone with me."

"Yet here you are trying to be alone with me."

My mouth drops open. Then I blow out a breath and hide behind my hands. "It's not like that," I muffle through my fingers.

"To be honest, I'm still trying to figure you out." He peers over the rim of his cup while enjoying a leisurely sip. "You tricked me into stepping out in the blizzard to proposition me."

I suck in breath. "I did no such thing!"

"You didn't make me an offer?"

"What? Not *that* kind of offer. What in the world, Mark? What kind of girl do you think I am?"

He blinks. "Proposition doesn't have to mean that."

"Since when?"

"Since always." He's annoyed.

Great.

I've annoyed the man I was hoping would save me. Leaning against the counter, coffee in one hand, he swipes around on his phone and then reads, "Proposition, verb: Fourteenth century, the action of proposing something to be done, to put forth, set forth, an offered plan of action." The snooty expression he slings my way says the rest. *I'm right. You're wrong, and what do you have to say for yourself now, woman?*

I furrow my brow. "It doesn't say anything about the

other thing?" I hate the way my voice grows high-pitched with nerves.

Surprise, surprise—Mark doesn't make eye contact as he tucks his phone away. "I skipped over that part."

"Ha! So, I'm right."

"No! Words can have very different meanings depending on context. You and I both know you didn't proposition me for... that. But nevertheless, you did proposition—set forth the offered plan of action—an outing of the two of us together. Tonight. Then when I tell you no, you—"

"You didn't tell me no this morning."

"Only because you bamboozled, hoodwinked, and hornswoggled all in one breath."

I'd take offense at his accusations, but he just said *hornswoggled*, and it's hilarious. Plus Mark has such a pleasant smile as he continues to rant that begs me to believe he's not too torn up about the whole thing. His gaze flits to the ceiling. "I was... lassoed, hogtied, and served on a platter."

"You done? And what's with the cowboy words?"

"Euphemisms."

Mark is exhausting. It's almost like he wants to be argued with. "I thought a euphemism was only for... other things."

"What other things?"

"You know, replacing words with other words when it's... distasteful."

"Who says this isn't distasteful? I've been shanghaied."

I tilt my head back with an audible sigh. "Staaahhhp."

"Then when I try to get out of it you mention stalker Dr. Kenny."

"Kendrick. He's not a—"

"You'd rather spend the evening with a stranger than this doctor. What's the deal?"

I fling my hands in the air. "Fine. If you don't want to go, you don't have to go. I will go by myself. Dr. Kendrick will think I invented a story that I had a date, he'll crowd me all evening, insist on fetching water and dessert, he'll try to dance with me, he'll whisper a running commentary of the evening's events, then I'll have to shake him off the next month at work. But it's fine. I'm a big girl and can handle it."

He releases a single grunt while setting down his coffee then recrosses his arms. "Try again."

I lift the tuxedo and slowly raise it toward him. Tightening my lips to keep away a grin, I do my best impression of a lost and lonely kitten. Mark hasn't seen nothing yet...

Big Eyes! Blink, blink, blink. Add in a pouty lip. Can I muster any tears? Lean into that tingle in my nose. Annnd there's some moisture. Almost there... A-ha.

I blink hard and feel the release of a single tear. Oh, the drama. Sniffle with a ragged intake of breath. "Please, Mark. I need help."

Mark lifts the side of his lip in a knowing smirk. "You are good. Give me that." He snatches the clothing and chucks it behind me to the table.

"Nickie, is it? Dr. Nickie...?"

"Brader." I smile, yet he only returns the stare. I say nothing else and wait for his response, letting the tear tickle all the way down my cheek. Staring contest champion over there, good heavens. Why is it so warm in this kitchen?

"What?" He speaks!

"My last name is Brader. I'm Dr. Brader."

"Huh. That's a fun trick." He chuckles. "I thought you were being weird and staring at me for no reason. We have the same last name."

"We do."

"What happens if I go with you tonight, then people think I'm your husband?"

"I guess you'd have to get me a ring." It takes a good amount of concentration to keep my expression chill. Am I… Did I… Am I flirting with Diana's cousin? It's way too much fun, and way easier than I thought it would be.

I should stop though.

We're too old to go on like this and it not mean something. I don't usually skip along the path, flirting with men. The men in town are either childhood friends that are already married—like Nathan—or we've already dated—like Gilbert—or I'm working hard to avoid—like Preston.

Then Mark arrives like a bowl of free chocolate, and suddenly I'm behaving like I don't have to be an adult, thinking, *Boy, wouldn't it be nice to have that ring.*

*She Didn't Need No Stinkin' Man* doesn't have to be the title of my memoir.

Mark's still staring, and I hope he isn't a mind reader.

Being single wasn't a rule. It was just one thing after another and then here I am delivering babies, lancing abscesses under toenails, reminding Grandpa to drink his MiraLAX with no extra time to attend singles bingo at the local coffee shop.

If I keep this up, I'll be Aunt Jewels in a few years. Retired and happy. Hosting house parties for the young'uns. The head of three different church committees. Which, I suppose, is really great. But… Her only family is a couple of nephews.

Did Jewel Conner choose the single life on purpose? What if I want to have my own baby and do the wife and mom thing? Still, Mark is decidedly *not* free candy. I shouldn't have asked this of him. So now, after propositioning the guy I met this morning for a ring—he's all Tommy Hilfiger relaxed against the kitchen counter—I wrack my brain attempting to formalize a fair response to let him out of the deal.

The corner of his mouth tugs into a slight smile. His hand stretches across the gap between us, and he wipes the tear from my face with the soft pad of his thumb.

It's nothing. It's everything. His touch is gentle, unhurried—like he's secure, and I haven't caught up yet.

I am a statue. Can I breathe? Oxygen. Who needs it?

Back against the counter, Mark takes an *I resign* sort of breath. "Dr. Brader, here's another plan, if you're willing."

Air fills my lungs, and my tense muscles relax.

"I'm looking for a wife this year."

"Ope! You what now?"

Mark rocks his head to one side. "Next year. Whatever. After the holidays when I'm back in Arizona, I'm all set to begin the process. So here's what I suggest. I, me, Mark Brader, offer to take you on a date. Not because I accidentally nodded at the wrong moment and you hooked me faster than a catfish on a nightcrawler. But it'll be good for me because I haven't taken anyone out in years. It'll be good for you, because of all the reasons you've already mentioned. But if we do this, I need you to understand I'm going because I decided I want to. And it'll be real. I'm not a stand-in."

Oxygen escapes in a whoosh. "Pardon, I must be more tired than I thought. Did Mark Brader ask me, a stranger, on a real date?"

"I did. I'll pick you up at five? And go take a nap. And you'd better wash your hair. You look terrible." It's not cute how he parrots my words from this morning.

Though he's not wrong. Self-consciously I pat the messy bun I secured around two a.m.

"What'll it be?" His question is direct, but he's smacked me with so much information I don't know what to answer first. Foremost is that I'm saved from going alone to the gala and will be shielded from the advances of Preston Kendrick. I'm clinging to that thought, and the relief is palpable.

But—Hold. The. Phone. Mark's *looking for a wife this year*. He's *set to begin the process*. Heck, no. "What just happened? I feel tricked. Professor Harold Hill convinced me to purchase a whole band with matching uniforms tricked."

"My credentials are better than Gary, Indiana, if you need a reference."

My head shakes no, and doesn't stop shaking, as I cast my eyes to the floor, noticing donut crumbs strewn under the chairs. His excuse about *looking for a wife and needs practice* is ludicrous. Yet Mark dropped a *Music Man* reference in answer to mine, so I'm willing to overlook ludicrous at this point.

"So why would you do this?" I peek in time to see him shrug.

"I decided it would be fun to go with you. You're funny. Direct. Kinda pretty. Since I'm going to start dating officially when I get home, it makes sense. I'm not interested in fake crap. Can I take you on a real date?"

"I'm—How—" Ugh, why are my thoughts so sluggish? Besides having worked all night. "What do you mean by a real date?" My mind zips to hand-holding and good-night kisses, but I'm not about to blab *Hey there, good lookin', are you planning to make-out with me, mister?*

"Can I call you Nickie? Nicole?"

"Nickie's fine."

"Look, Nickie, don't make this complicated. I'm single. You're single. We're two, compatible strong-willed adults. I'm interested in spending time with you. We dress up, eat fancy food, do whatever it is people do at hospital fundraiser gala things. I'm sure we'll have a good time. I go home to Arizona. You in?"

I nod, gaze unfocused. "You played me like a fiddle at a barn dance." My voice is a soft, unsure whisper.

"Let me walk you to your car, ma'am. You're sure Grandpa's good here?" He jerks a thumb to the living room where I've completely forgotten other humans exist. Mark gently takes my wrist and threads it through his crooked elbow. "Caught in a whirlwind of charm and trickery."

"Um... Seized tighter than the first meal of a starving anaconda escaped from the science lab?"

"Eww, don't be morbid." The warmth of his arm against mine is lovely. "You'd wriggle out of this if you didn't want to go."

Maybe he doesn't know me as well as he thinks he does. I pull him to a stop as we come to the door. "Mark, jokes aside. Let's get this straight. If this is real, but you live super far away, what do we even tell people?"

"It's none of their business. Does it matter?"

"It's Hadley Springs. What do we say when they ask who you are?"

"We're not fabricating a story, if that's what you mean. Introduce me as your date or Diana's cousin, or *Mark Brader*." He leans closer like two spies.

"Ha. But what if they ask where you're from?"

"I'm visiting from Phoenix."

"I know!"

"Then why are you asking? It's way past your bedtime.

We'll talk later. I don't want to go out with a zombie. Please go home and sleep."

I stare at the door handle. Do I simply drive home? Mark is going to take me out on a real date. What if he ditches at the last minute? Why is he doing this? Why do I care since this is what I asked him to do earlier? While standing in the snow an hour ago, I didn't think through the repercussions.

Mark's hand waves in front of my face. "You know what? I'm driving you home."

I glance into his chocolate eyes, and my shoulders relax. "That's not necessary. My car's right out front."

"I'll drive you home in your car, bring it back here, and then I'll pick you up... in your car." He flashes a cheesy grin that hints at the ridiculousness of this situation. "Otherwise we're going in the mini-van, because Nate's hatchback hasn't left the garage in days because of a flat tire."

"Are you really this—" I'm a fish with no tongue when my gaze trips on the scene before me. *Glub, glub, glub.* What are words?

As Mark bends to slip his feet into a pair of black tennis shoes, his shirt slips a few inches exposing a toned side. The edge of a swirling tattoo peeks from the hem of the shirt. "Am I really this what?" He straightens. Stomps his foot into the shoe then rifles through a wall of coats hung on the hooks beside the door.

I will not fixate on what I didn't see. I will not— What was it? A wave? Words? It'd better not be a skull. What if it's Latin?

"Come on, Doctor. Let's get you to bed."

My eyes widen at his choice of words, and I'm sure I see the hint of a smirk before he leads me into the snowy outdoors.

# MARK

VULFPECK—BACKPOCKET

It's been a long time since I had a chance to suit up, and I look forward to the evening away from the commotion of the Weston household. While I sit at the table letting Lauren fix my hair, Nathan slings advice from the living room, where he's bouncing Jack on a knee with Lisa on his foot and the twins crowding his lap.

"If she asks how she looks, the answer is 'stunning.' No hesitation. Doesn't matter if she resembles a tablecloth with sparkles."

I shake my head with a chuckle.

"Dad! That's mean. Nickie's going to look amazing." Lauren grips the sides of my face. "Hold still, I'm almost done." Her small fingers comb through my hair.

I'm afraid I'll look like a teen pop star before she's finished. There's a collection of products on the edge of the table, and I've lost count of what she's put into my hair, but she insists she knows what she's doing—and I guess I don't really care. It's worth it to see Lauren energized over this. I love seeing her feel accomplished and proud of something.

Lauren's a completely different girl right now than the one struggling with math this morning. Amazing to witness the passion and determination Lauren has for these creative pursuits.

"If you can't dazzle her with charm, then at least be useful—offer to hold her purse." Nathan's *advice* has only gotten more ridiculous.

"I'm not holding her purse. Have you seen what some girls carry? It'll be as sparkly as the dress."

Diana barks a laugh from where she's putting together enchiladas for dinner. "Then you better dazzle her with charm. And sit up straight. You're an editor, not a goblin."

This is turning out to be more than I bargained for. "I'm joining her for a work event. Don't make more of it than it is."

"If you spill anything on your jacket, take it off," Lauren offers. "You look great without it."

I narrow my eyes at the kid. "Since when do you get to offer dating advice?"

Diana opens the oven door and releases a blast of warm air. "Don't forget: Left foot, right foot." She stands and arches her back in a side-to-side stretch. "Slow dancing is easy—it's not a wrestling match."

"No one said anything about dancing. Hospital Fundraiser Gala Thing. I did not agree to take anyone dancing."

"Be a gentleman," Diana commands. "Open doors. Pull out her chair. Don't double dip the appetizers."

I roll my eyes and mock Diana with a "mi-mi-mi..." until Lauren and I are laughing together.

Nathan enters with Lisa in one arm and Jack in the other. "If there's a chocolate fountain, pace yourself."

Diana snorts a laugh. "Don't correct her grammar unless you want to dance by yourself."

"Correct her grammar." I wink at Lauren. "Check."

"Oh!" Nathan is making eyes at Diana instead of me. I begin to see this is a game between the two of them. "Don't text in front of her then laugh at a separate conversation. Girls hate that."

"Turn your phone off completely." Diana steps closer to Nathan. "You won't need it because you're going to flatter her with your undivided attention."

"Good one." Nathan edges toward his wife. "Also, don't use the word 'roaches' in conversation, ever."

Diana nods emphatically. "Or phlegm." She ticks off her fingers. "Mucus, crevice, puke, or vomit."

"Or cornucopia," Nathan says, dead-serious.

"And that's why I love you." Diana kisses Nathan on the mouth then turns to me. "Mark, listen up." She places both palms on the table and leans over it. "Do not, under any circumstances, mention *Project: Find a Wife*." She lifts a hand when I start to ask how she knows about that. "You left your notebook on the table, and I read through it before putting it in your room. I don't care if Nickie checks every single one of your boxes. Don't tell her you're looking for a wife."

Her arms cross and then make a swiping *safe* motion. "Doesn't matter how excited I am for the two of you, don't mention your plan. Don't TMI about anything deep." There she goes with the counting fingers again. "Don't talk about your dead cat from second grade. Don't give her advice she's not asking for."

"Don't talk about the dead cat. Got it. Lauren, we good

up there?" I roll my eyes skyward. No reason to tell Diana the deed's already done. "It's time I get out of here."

Lauren steps away and scrutinizes her work. "It's perfect."

I shrug into the borrowed jacket that fits surprisingly well. "If you are quite finished with these priceless words of wisdom, I have one major request. Please, I'm begging you, do not mention this to Cordy. She'll get excited about nothing and hound me with questions. So can we all be cool and mind our own business? Hmm?" I eye Diana until she nods. Nathan shrugs, and Lauren twitches her lips side to side. "Lauren, can you keep this to yourself?"

"Like a surprise?"

"Something like that."

"Then you'll tell Aunt Cordy later, when you're engaged?"

Nathan clears his throat and escapes into the other room, failing to hide a burst of laughter.

But Lauren isn't making a joke.

I kneel in front of her and take her hand. "Nickie and I just met today. We're getting to know each other as friends. That's all we're doing."

"But Mom said you were getting married." Her gaze bounces from me to her mom. "She said not to tell Nickie, but you're getting married. I think it's a great idea. You and Nickie are really smart and super nice. Like, the two most wonderful people that I know."

Wow, her praise hits me in all the right places, and I pull her into a hug. "Thanks, I think you're really super nice and wonderful too." I steady myself as I hold her away from me, hands on her shoulders.

I've always been honest with Lauren. Maybe it's the oldest child in her, or the way we've connected since she was a baby. Not having any siblings of my own, Diana's kids are my only chance at enjoying nieces or nephews. There's a seed of wisdom in Lauren that will someday grow into maturity.

Her round blue eyes are deeply trusting, and I refuse to offer anything but the honest truth. "I want nothing more than to get married and have a bunch of kids just like you. But tonight's not about that. Don't put too much thought into it, okay? We're two people hanging out." I squeeze her shoulders. "I'm glad Nickie has your approval though. That means a lot to me, but we can't know the future."

"Well." Lauren gently adjusts a section of my hair. "Hurry up and get to know each other because I only get to be a flower girl when I'm small and cute."

"I'll remember that. Now, run tell Grandpa Jeffrey it's time to go. He and Landon are playing Risk in the boys' room."

Once I get him into the car, Grandpa hums show tunes as we slowly make our way across town in Nickie's Honda. I catch the melody, and when I join him in a round of "Oh What a Beautiful Morning" from *Oklahoma!* he gains confidence and belts out each word. Before long there's a grand smile plastered across the old man's face.

"You've got a nice set of lungs, Jeffrey."

"Not bad yourself, Curly," he says with a smile. "I played Ali Hakim my senior year of high school."

"Sorry, remind me who that is?"

"*Oklahoma!* traveling salesman. Flirting with all the ladies."

We arrive in front of the house. "Is that how you wooed Mrs. Jeffrey?" I unbuckle and wait for him to find his cane.

He adjusts his collar in preparation to open the door.

"Joyce was the student-teacher who directed that year. She's the only reason I went out for the show."

"Grandpa Jeffrey! Holy moly, there's a story."

He chuckles. "All above board. I was already nineteen and didn't ask her out until the night of graduation."

"And she said yes?"

"She shut the door in my face and called me a child. I puttered around for another six months before I tried again."

"And then she said yes?"

"I have two grandchildren, so it appears that she did. Quit gabbing and get over here and help me out of this car."

"Yes, sir." I raise my collar and tug my winter gloves tighter as I walk around to his side. Soft flakes of snow drift from the starless sky. The street lights are already glowing this winter evening. White twinkle lights wrap around the railings and posts of the porch. It's not extravagant, but the holiday cheer makes the place festive along with a wreath tied with a red ribbon on the blue front door.

We're nearing the door when it opens, and a smiling Nickie waves us forward in a shimmering gown of baby-blue. The dress is for grown-ups. Very nice. Womanly... and —I swallow—tight. Slinky? Flowy? Like a... Adjectives skitter around my empty brain like roaches running from a spotlight.

Nope. Not supposed to think about roaches.

Or puke.

The long sleeves of her slinky, flowy, shimmering, tight outfit must not be very warm because her body trembles in a full shiver, and she rubs her hands together. Jeffrey whacks his cane against my shin, and that's my cue to quit standing here like an idiot.

I step forward with the man holding my arm, and

Nickie shuts the door behind us. Um, she looks like a really pretty thing.

"You look like a fish." I sputter. Words slip from my tongue unedited. I catch her confused expression and rush to clarify. "One of those shiny ones with the scales."

Her confusion twists into a laugh. "Ha! Thank you. I think." She runs her hands down her waist and over her hips, drawing attention to them, as if the dress needed smoothing. "I'm going to walk away. Okay? I'm going to take a second over there, then I'm going to come back so you can try that again. Mmk? Maybe you do need practice. Gather your thoughts, mister."

She twirls her finger in the air with a smirk. "I'm going now. Get it together, Mark. Round two—here we go. *Exeunt.*"

Grandpa mutters, "Beautiful, amazing, gorgeous, breathtaking—"

"Yeah. Got it. Gimme a second." I shake out my hands and close my eyes, breathing the warm smells of the house. Stale coffee. Cinnamon. Something girly. Fresh snow. I tug off my gloves and give them to Grandpa.

"You ready?" Nickie hollers from somewhere down the hall. "Places, everyone."

"Action!" Grandpa answers.

Nickie sashays into the hallway, a compelling smile lighting her face, her gaze focused on my reaction. I take my time letting my gaze travel from the soft blond curls pulled on top of her head with a few positioned around her face, to the shoulder-to-shoulder neckline that reminds me of a ballerina leotard, down her arms to she pointed end that loops around each middle finger. The sparkles glimmer in snowflake patterns across her torso. The skirt blends into a darker blue that swishes into a waterfall around her legs to brush the wooden floor, hiding her heels that click against the wood.

As she approaches she lifts a hand to me. I take it, but instead of raising it to my lips, which is what I think she was after, I drag her the next step closer as I move toward her.

I've been given a second chance. I'll not waste it.

The moment slows. If I were filming, the camera would zoom on her doe-eyed expression with flawless makeup that extends her eyelashes. Emboldened by the fun of this woman and her show, I slip my hand behind her neck and press my lips against hers in a gentle kiss. Slowly, before releasing her, I whisper against her mouth. "You're stunning."

When I break contact, she furrows her brows and flicks her gaze to Grandpa and back at me. "Good. Yep. Thaaat's fine then. Thank you." She clears her throat. "You are—look good too. Very nice. Suit fits. You're no Captain von Trapp, but you'll do. I suppose. That's good. Yep. Perfect. Come on in. Grandma wants to meet you before we go. She's right over, um." Nickie claps her hands and turns as if that will fix the jumbled mess pouring from her mouth. "Come on in. Grandpa, you, ah, you had a good day?"

I glance at Grandpa to gauge his reaction, and he offers a solid thumbs-up before dropping my gloves on the floor to follow Nickie down the hall. "I did, at that. Played Risk all afternoon. Almost won."

# NICKIE

FLOWER DRUM SONG—I ENJOY BEING A GIRL

"Thank you again for shoveling all of this." I take Mark's offered hand and let him guide me down the porch steps. After he brought me home this morning, he'd immediately surveyed the sidewalk and asked for the shovel. However much I didn't want to make him do my chores, I was too grateful to fuss. "I wish I could have helped you, but I had strict instructions not to turn into a zombie."

"Who normally takes care of it? Have you looked into hiring a service?"

I appreciate the support of his steady hand as I carefully place each foot along the sidewalk. "My brother handles it. John's unfortunately stuck in Omaha today."

"Ah, well it was my pleasure to help out."

"I bet it was actually. You seem to be a really nice guy."

"A nice guy." He mumbles the phrase. "Do I get a certificate with that?"

We pause beside my red Honda. "What do you mean?"

"A participation certificate. I can frame it and hang it on

the wall." Mark brackets his thumb and forefinger in the air as he pretends to read. "Mark Brader: A Nice Guy."

"Har har har. You're so funny." I release his hand to open the driver's door.

"What are you doing?" He pushes the door shut. "Your seat's over there."

"This is my car."

His hand on my elbow tugs me away. "I'm driving."

I let him walk me around, my very high heels wobbling on the salted concrete. "It's my car."

"I'm driving."

To South Pacific's well-known tune, I sing, "I'm gonna wash that man right out of my car. I'm gonna wash that man right out of my car, and send him on his way."

Without any hesitation he opens the passenger door. "Get in."

Apparently, breaking into random parodied lyrics doesn't faze him. The door is now between us and with my incredible shoes, I meet him eye to eye. I don't mind letting him drive. But why does he insist? There's no reason to yank me around. If this is a real date—as he implies it definitely is—I won't pretend to go along with this chauvinistic behavior just so a man can feel good about himself.

I could go with Preston if I want to be treated this way.

Consciously relaxing my face clear of irritation, I offer a smile with my best bedside manner skills in place. "Mark, I'm very happy to let you drive. You don't need to strut."

He blinks, a bit of surprise showing in his face. "I'm giving off Dr. Kenny vibes!" He sucks in cold air through his teeth in a grimace. "Sorry. You're completely right. I still have your keys, and I let it go to my head—"

I place my hand against his chest to calm him. "It's okay."

Covering my hand with his, he says, "Nickie, it would be a great honor if you'd allow me to drive this evening. And..." He moves our hands on top of the open door and leans forward.

Pulled by the tension, I lean closer, waiting for whatever else he's about to share.

"I miss driving because I don't have a car in Arizona."

"There's a bit of interesting news." We draw nearer over the door, our hands sandwiched together.

His throat bobs with a swallow before a grin stretches his lips.

"You may drive." I duck into the seat and shut the door so fast that it slams because he didn't even hide his desire to kiss me again.

The crazy thing is that I wouldn't hate it.

I focus on adjusting my dress and pulling on the seat-belt. Passenger Princess is settled. I really don't care who drives as long as nobody pushes me around. Two kisses before the date even begins is unnecessary. Whatever would Grandma Joyce say?

Mark zips around the front and slides into the driver's seat.

"You don't have a car." Aghast, I clutch a string of invisible pearls. "Are you sure you're capable?"

"Har har har." He starts the engine before catching me with a flirtatious side grin. "Who's the funny one now? I don't have a car because I live in a big ol' city, and I get to pay people to drive me around. It's more efficient to outsource. But trust me, I'm very capable."

"Aren't we fancy." My reply was injected with mockery, but as I think about it, that doesn't sound so bad. A chauffeur would be fun. I imagine a driver coming to the house. All I do is sit in the back and think or read. "What a life."

This man takes up too much room beside me. It's exciting. A first date. A real one. A real first date. How long has it been? Years. A decade. Too long. "I've never been on a date with an adult," I speak quickly, laying the truth out before we've left the driveway in case he wants to change his mind.

Mark's forehead creases as he stares at the dashboard. He shakes his head as if to clear his thoughts and then laughs. "I think that needs a re-write." He continues to chuckle under his breath and angles toward me, placing his hand on my seat-back with an open, expectant expression. "Please. I don't think you meant to say what you just said. You've never been on a date with an adult?"

Were I with anyone else, I would be immediately embarrassed at my poor choice of words and that incriminating confession. But oddly enough, Mark's smile makes me want to laugh about it too. Maybe saying dumb things in front of each other is our thing now. My lower lip slips between my teeth as I shy away from his gaze. "I seem to be stumbling over my words more than usual."

"Sometimes words are hard. But take your time. Please, try again."

The art of *thinking* is its own sport with his hand on the back of my seat, and his full attention waiting for my next words. "I... haven't... been on a real date since I started college."

"How is that possible? You're really pretty."

"Like a fish?"

He grins. "With scales." Fully rotating his torso, right hand still on my seat, he looks out the rear window as he backs out of the driveway. "I told you words are hard sometimes." Then he mutters, "I can't believe you drive a car older than Lauren."

"Runs fine. We can't all live like millionaires with chauffeurs."

"You'd be surprised." He slowly accelerates onto the street. "Tally what you spend on insurance, gas, oil, maintenance, the initial purchase." He shrugs, casual. "You add all that up, and I guarantee it's more than what I spend on drivers that I order anytime I need them. Plus, I redeem the time by knocking out a few more chapters. Same reason I live in a hotel. I win on all accounts."

"You live in a what?"

"A hotel."

"On purpose? Let me guess, it's more efficient?"

"Absolutely. With one bill I've outsourced breakfast, internet, housekeeping, gym, pool, hot-tub, lawn care." He rattles off the list and relaxes in his seat, one hand on the wheel. "Luxury living with no long term lease, mortgage, or property taxes."

"Huh. You're an editor. Right?"

"Right. And you're a doctor."

"We're practically the same."

"Except if you mess up, people die. If I mess up, people get bad books?"

I can't help but laugh. "See? We're the same."

Mark's smile is clear in the dashboard lights. "I like you, Nickie."

His words crash like a rock through a window. So unexpected. I want to tell him he's wrong. He doesn't know me, how could he say such things?

*Relax.* It was a generic compliment. He probably likes ice cream too. I'm sure he doesn't mean too much by it. We just met for heaven's sake! Sure, he's cute. He's funny. He has a secret tattoo and *whatever*, but a kiss at the door and a confession of his feelings before dinner? I'd better be careful, or he'll carry my heart to Phoenix.

A few seconds of silence stretch between us, the tires quiet on the snow-covered street. From the corner of my eye I notice him glance at me, then back to the road. Then me again. "Everything okay?"

The man is nice *and* observant.

Overthinking never improves the moment, so I smile and push down that flare of concern. "Tell me about Arizona."

"It's south of here. A bit warmer." He slows at a stop sign and carefully turns left at the intersection.

I realize I never told him where the venue was located. "How do you know where we're going?"

"I looked it up."

Nice, observant, *and* forward thinking. Mark is becoming more attractive by the second.

"Tell me, Nickie, what did you mean about not going out since college? Was that intentional on your part?"

"Or am I secretly a huge loser? Ha. No. Yes? No, I wasn't intentionally being a loser. Yes, I was too busy and said no all the time to everyone about everything. Unless it was going to help me graduate sooner, I avoided it. I was a shootin' star. Pew!"

"Defying the laws of gravity." Mark states Queen's lyrics as fact.

"Like Lady Godiva." I think about the few men I've spent much time with, and can't help but compare them to Mark. I'm beginning to see that Mark is exactly as he appears to be. Despite the humor, he's not playing an angle. If he says he likes me, it's probably because he simply, well, likes me. I ask, "Do you quote all lyrics or just 80's rock?"

"All of them. It's a curse. Cordy and I can go entire

conversations on lyrics. Welcome to the club. Sorry, back to you. You were too busy to date. Then what?"

"Yeah, so I took as many classes as allowed. I'm young for my grade in the first place and moved into the dorms the day after my eighteenth birthday. Add in the dual credits I earned in high school, maxed out semesters and summer school—I blasted through my undergrad in two-and-a-half years. Oh, no. Did I just confirm how much of a loser I really am?" I duck my face into my hands, embarrassed that the explanation feels more like bragging. Super nerd, right here!

"That's incredible." Mark pushes my hands away from my face without fully taking his gaze from the road. "Don't be embarrassed about being too smart to mess around. So, you're twenty years old with an undergrad, then what?"

"Then the real work began. I was on the accelerated track and finished medical school in three years instead of four, all that was left was a few years of residency."

"Why the rush?"

"I ask myself that every day, Mark. As a seventeen-year-old, that plan made perfect sense. I was aiming for Doctors without Borders, or mission work, or something adventurous. Blasted through school and was making money as a family practitioner by the time I was twenty-five. Why take eleven full years like everyone else, when I could do it in eight? I always told myself the sooner I finished school, the sooner I could start my real life."

I breathe, telling myself that I've shared enough. But if we're being honest, I may as well get it all out. "So, here I am, thirty-two, living my real life, and wondering what I missed. When Grandma and Grandpa needed the help and Mom and Dad weren't in a financial position to step away from their work, I didn't have the luxury to rest on the weekends. But I wish I would have been more available for my family those years I was in school. There's nothing I'm doing now that justifies the means." My voice hitches, and I swallow the emotions that almost take over.

Lock that up, girl. This is a first date not therapy.

Mark doesn't rush to respond, and his expression gives away nothing. His thumb taps once on the steering wheel, then three times. "Sounds like you have regrets."

I release a quiet laugh and glance out the window, the headlights barely illuminating the snow-covered field on my side of this arrow-straight country road. "Regret is a strong word."

"Remorse? Sorrow?"

"Those are worse!" I huff, part exasperation, part amusement. "Hang on, let me think." I yank off my gloves and rub my cold hands together, suddenly aware of the chill still in the car. My hands are freezing, though I'm afraid my armpits are sweating. "I rushed through my twenties so I could hurry up and get on with life, and now I feel..." My words trail off as heat pricks behind my eyes. "Oh, great. Nevermind. The word that comes immediately to mind isn't what I want to share."

I reach for the vent, adjusting the direction, then fiddle with the collar of my wool peacoat like it suddenly needs all my attention. Mark doesn't condemn or insist I answer. Even so. "Shame." I admit the truth barely above a whisper. "Shame for wasted years. The best work I'm doing is taking care of my grandparents, and I didn't need eleven years of school for that."

The silence stretches long enough that I feel stupid for opening my mouth. I look ahead, blinking fast, pretending the snowflakes outside are more interesting than the vulnerability inside the car.

Mark focuses on the icy road while methodically removing his right glove. With a slight glance, he covers my hand on my lap, burrowing his fingers into my fist until I relax into his hold. I stare at our joined hands as the shared warmth seeps into me.

I wasn't looking for this.

This morning, all I wanted was a way around an annoying, perhaps stressful, evening. The peace from this connection can't be so real so soon.

I blow a raspberry. "Whatever. After saying it out loud, that's a pretty strong word, and I think I'd like to go back to talking about fish. Or, donuts or something."

"Shame *off* you. Those years weren't wasted." Mark hums softly and squeezes my hand. "Now, we have shrimp puffs to conquer. What do you need from me tonight? I can hype-girl you in front of Kenny, we can ignore him or make him jealous, make out in front of your boss. It's whatever you want—I'm game."

"Mark!" I laugh out his name and shove his hand back in his lap. "Behave yourself."

10

## MARK



It's in a barn. Hospital Fundraiser Gala Thing is in a barn. In December. In Nebraska.

I'm not even surprised. With Hadley Springs boasting a thousand citizens, there's not much call for an event center. Having grown up in small-town Nebraska myself, I understand that if they want to keep it local, it's either this, the senior center, or the high school gym.

"Oh, Mark, look." Nickie points to the rows of twinkle lights secured by foot-high posts that lead us along the sidewalk. "It's so pretty."

"So pretty," I parrot. "As pretty as a troll ensconced in a beauty parlor. Where do you think they stashed the cows for the evening?"

"You said you would behave." She says that, but with her teasing smile and shoulder bumping into mine I'm not so sure that she wants me to.

I put my arm around her waist and guide her closer.

"You telling me to behave isn't the same as me agreeing to it."

At the door, we're greeted by an older gentleman who takes Nickie's coat. I didn't wear one because all I have is a neon yellow ski jacket. The tux was warm enough. We join a quickly moving line of other well-dressed couples in a small foyer.

"Dr. Brader!" The screech comes from a young female in a short red dress high-stepping across the hallway on the toes of her matching heels. "You're heeere!"

Nickie slides one foot forward on the carpet and subtly leans closer to me. I sense danger and rest a hand on her back.

"Hey, Christy. So good to see you again." Nickie offers a hand, but Christy barrels into a hug. If I weren't supporting Nickie, they both would have tumbled over. An instant later, Christy stands in front of me.

"Who's this? Hi."

"Hello, I'm—"

"Mr. Brader." Nickie interjects and hides her left hand around my back. "You haven't met him yet, have you? This is Mr. Brader."

"Your brother?" Christy sounds possessively hopeful.

I pull Nickie against my side, slipping my hand around her back to rest on the curve of her hip. "Afraid not. You must be thinking of John. I'm Mark Brader, not the brother."

"Oh, I didn't even know you were married. We have a table over in the back if you want to join us. Okay. See you — Oh! Brian's here!" And Christy scuttles to the door to accost someone else.

"That's the plan? Huh?" I look into Nickie's guilty face. "Is this where we get to make out?"

"*Psh*, Mark." She pushes against my chest and steps away, but I catch her elbow.

After running my hand down the length of her arm, I thread our fingers together. "Stay," I scold. "You don't get to call all the shots tonight. Who was that? And why am I now your husband?"

Before she answers, we're at the registration table and a woman in a sleek black dress hands me a pen. "Hi, so glad you joined us tonight. Oh, hello, Nicole. I have your seat reserved at the table nearest the microphone. We'll be able to start in about ten minutes. Do you need anything else?"

"That'll be fine, Wilma. Did Dr. Gyle arrive yet? I was worried about him getting here through the snow." Nickie releases my hand and takes the pen from me.

"Afraid not, honey. Nobody from Omaha was able to make it tonight." Wilma adjusts the gold wire rim of her oversized glasses. "We should have canceled." Leaning closer to keep her voice between the three of us, she continues. "Since the senator was already on the road south of the storm, we couldn't afford to adjust his schedule, and you know the hassle we've had with the caterers."

Nickie answers with a variety of polite noises as Wilma continues to list the reasons the gala is still on despite yesterday's blizzard.

Christy is hanging on Brian's arm while he tries to hand over his coat. The poor kid is mousetrapped. His mouth smiles, but panic reflects in his eyes. Brian doesn't look much older than eighteen and glances over his shoulder at an older couple, perhaps his parents.

"With Tom running the live-streaming, we hope a few of the more affluent guests will still chime in." Wilma clasps her hands together as if that's that.

"Sounds like a great plan," Nickie says while signing

our names on a single line of the sheet: *Dr. Nicole and Mark Brader*.

I tighten my lips against a smile. It's her mess to clean if tongues start wagging, not mine. The moment Nickie sets down the pen she fumbles for my hand.

Leading her away from the table, I ask, "You okay? You seem nervous."

"Yeah, I forgot how *much* this night is. What do you think about the schedule change? I think we should do one together to fill in the time."

"Sure. You're going to be okay?" I tug her from the path of an excited Christy as she leads Brian ahead of us, bypassing the line. "Did you get enough sleep today?"

Nickie waves at someone else across the entryway but speaks to me. "Not enough to stand up to Christy apparently. That would have been you." She nods to the passing couple. "She's the senator's daughter. She's seventeen and —" Nickie purses her lips. "She's delightful."

"You're delightful." My compliment bounces off of Nickie, which makes me want to keep dropping them until she hears me. Doesn't matter if I never see her again, there's no reason we can't have fun tonight.

"Whatever." She squeezes my hand. "What song should we do?"

"For what?"

"The lip-sync competition."

"Of course." I straighten my shoulders with forced assurance. That must be what I accidentally agreed to with a simple, *sure*. I'd plead ignorance, that I was distracted by Christy and Brian, but the truth is... Nickie. She overpowers my guard.

The spyglass flings from my grip, and she's breached the tower before I catch a glimpse. Before I can plan, I'm overrun. At this point, I'm already here, overdressed in a penguin suit, standing next to the most beautiful woman letting out rumors that I'm somebody special. She wants a show, and I'm gladly the jester before her throne.

"Let's go sit down," I say with a smile. This evening just got a whole lot more fun.

We enter the main room, and I'm taken aback by the transformation. The outside is an old barn covered in lights, yet in here there's a concrete floor stained with swirls of tans and browns. Dim lights from multiple chandeliers cast a soft orange glow. About thirty round tables with silver-colored tablecloths form a loose U shape with a DJ in one corner, the caterer in the other. Soft instrumental music sets a romantic mood to the place as women in flowing dresses flitter about hugging each other, while men in suits try to keep up.

It's nice but a little stuffy. Aside from Christy, most of the guests are significantly older than us. I look over at Nickie, and she's chewing her bottom lip while her gaze roams the crowd.

I swipe her hair behind her ear, and whisper, "I want to kiss you again."

"Mark!" Nickie furtively looks around as if we'll be caught. "You can't say things like that."

"I can, and I did. Did you mean *shall* not? Or *may* not?" And there I go, correcting grammar.

"You're confusing me because I don't know what the rules are."

"*May* is asking or giving permission. *Can* is reserved for—"

"Did you bring a PowerPoint? I'll take notes. I meant dating rules."

"Ah, where's the handbook? I'll read it."

She holds my gaze, and I can almost see the energy swirling around in her brain, trying to decide what she wants.

"I want to help you have fun." I rub my thumb over the back of her hand in mine. "What can I do?"

"I don't want to make this something it's not." Says the woman clinging to my hand and spreading rumors we're married.

"Then tell me what you want."

"I want you to kiss me too, but that's not the point, so knock it off."

Releasing her hand with a chuckle, I back away. "Got it, but remember that I'm not the one telling stories about us." Unless the room is filled with out-of-town guests, I'm not sure what she thinks will happen. I flutter the fingers of my left hand then gesture toward the podium by the DJ. "Go get our seats. It looks like there's a bar over there. You want anything?"

"Lemon drop martini. Sugar rim."

"Candy in a cup for the Sugar Plum Fairy. Makes sense."

It's hard to wipe the smile off my face as we separate. Even though I'm not exactly sure what I've gotten myself into tonight, I guarantee it'll be fun.

11

---

# NICKIE

OKLAHOMA! SOUNDTRACK—PEOPLE WILL SAY WE'RE IN LOVE

Standing by my seat, I review my cue cards for the welcome. It's not much of a speech though it's the official start of the evening. Wilma went over the adjustments to the schedule and double checked that I had the updated announcements. I flip to the second card and look over the main points. Guests of interest. Silent auction. After I open the evening, we'll move right into dinner, Tom will play the recording sent in from Dr. Gyle, I'll introduce the DJ, who runs the lip-sync competition and opens the floor for dancing, then Wilma finalizes the auction. All good.

I check the clock on my phone. It's time. Shaking out my arms, I breathe long and deep. With a practiced smile, I step behind the microphone. "Welcome and good evening."

My voice echoes through the banquet hall. Mark smiles from where he's in line at the bar. I hold his gaze until he winks. Quickly I look away before he flusters me, and I give guests a few more seconds to end their conversations. When most are turned toward me, I continue my little speech.

There's a collective sigh of disappointment at the change of schedule for the missing Dr. Gyle, but people excite again when I remind them of the lip-sync competition.

"Is Tom here? Tom and Lenny?" I ask. There's some shoving and hooting from a back corner of the room. Our only two male nurses from the clinic made a big splash last year with their performance of "Electric Avenue." They must have spent weeks working on a dance routine for it. "There they are, our reigning champions. What do you have prepared for us this year?"

Tom shouts above the noise, "Check back in an hour!"

I laugh with the crowd. "You heard it folks, guess we'll have to wait and see. Now if you'll go ahead and find your seats, dinner is served. Rose will dismiss each table when it's your turn. Wave your hand, Rose. There she is. Again, we're so grateful for everyone's support, and I hope you have a wonderful evening."

Done.

I step carefully to my table, holding my smile until I'm back in my seat. Public speaking doesn't really make me nervous, but I still find my heart beating faster than it should and my hand trembles as I smooth the silver and grey tablecloth.

"A vision in blue." The compliment startles me. Then Preston pulls out the chair beside me. "This spot open?" Before I answer, he's seated.

"Hey Preston, how are you?" I find Mark across the room. He's laughing with the man standing in line with him at the small bar. He's warm, attentive, and apparently hilarious.

"Who're you smiling at?" Preston leans closer to follow my line of sight.

"Sorry, I was distracted." I force my attention back to

the table. I'd love to point out Mark with *Behold, I brought a date! I didn't fabricate a man! Isn't he hot?* But I won't brag. Mark will be over here soon enough. "What were you saying? Are you here with anyone tonight?"

"Not really."

Mark catches my eye and lifts his chin in acknowledgment. I look away, feeling my skin prickle at being caught staring at him. Again.

"You look fantastic." Preston's eyes are puffy with lack of sleep as he observes my updo and shimmering dress. He taps a finger to a crystal clip I have secured in my hair. "Snow queen. I like it."

"Thank you, it's not every day we get out of the pajamas."

"I hear you, there. May as well make the best of it." He leans toward me. "You should have seen Darren when he heard you were bringing a date."

I breathe in slowly and try not to show how his nearness makes me uncomfortable. "It's not really any of Darren's business." Our office manager keeps careful tabs on everything and everyone at the clinic. He's so by-the-book it borders on OCD, but we're lucky to have him. And he usually stays in his lane. Preston's the one who had no business talking about me at work.

Mark weaves around the tables with one drink and holds my gaze until he's beside me. "Hey babe, thanks for your patience. The guy didn't have a clue about your drink order, but he said to give this a try. If you don't like it, I'll take it back." He slides a short glass toward me.

"You didn't get anything for yourself?"

"Nah, I don't drink. And I got so busy talking with Trenton I actually forgot to ask about a soda. You know Trenton?"

"I don't. Where's he from?"

Preston clears his throat. "Trenton Brown? He's taking over his dad's seed company. Massive donors to local charities. They probably own half the corn fields in our county."

Mark smiles and offers his hand across the table in front of me to Preston. "Hi, I'm Mark."

"Dr. Kendrick. Nice to meet you."

If Mark's surprised, he doesn't show it. He must have known though. That's probably why he threw out the pet name. I pinch my lips against a smile. What's real and what's fake has blurred, and I'm not sure where we stand.

Mark plops in his seat, completely comfortable. "So, lip-sync competition. Let's plan."

My phone lights with a text message, and I notice two missed calls from Mom. "Hang on. This might be—"

> Mom: Please call me! Grandma's
> unresponsive.

Mark must have read the text over my shoulder because he's suddenly standing, keys in hand. "I'll get the car. Kendrick, take over anything else she's responsible for tonight."

"What's going on?" Preston asks as Mark disappears.

"It's Grandma, she's—" I fumble to unlock my phone. "I need to go." I stand on shaking legs and swipe up the text notification. Preston is walking beside me, hand on my elbow, clearing the path until I'm in the entryway. "Mom says she's unresponsive." The call rings with no answer, each ring more painful than the last until Mom's voicemail picks up. I jam my thumb onto the red button with a frustrated exhale.

Preston has my coat around my shoulders and leads me outside. Mark's already waiting at the end of the sidewalk with my car. Door open, Preston and Mark converse as I send another outgoing call. Mark crouches beside me outside the car. "Notecards?"

"What?" I glance away from the phone and notice the lines skating across Mark's normally smooth forehead.

He takes my clutch from my lap, finds the cards I used for my speech, and hands them to Preston. By the time Mom's voicemail answers again, I notice that I'm buckled, and we've left the parking lot.

Phone cradled in my lap, I stare into the blowing snow in the dark evening. My heart's doing something ridiculous, and I can't keep my mind on any one clear thought. It's not panic. It's not fear exactly. It's a heartache that I've only felt a few times. It's a vice that restricts oxygen. Without the emotional wall I build each time I step into the office, it's a pain I wasn't prepared for tonight. I knew this day would come, but it wasn't supposed to be today.

Not today. And not tomorrow. And not—

Mark's hand covers my clenched fingers, and his voice clears my fog. He's praying and although the words make sense, I can't follow the sentences. Regardless, whatever he says has power. My lungs release. I drop my head against the seat, eyes closed, nothing in my thoughts but *please, please, please...*

# 12

## MARK

### MONDAY, DECEMBER 25

SWITCHFOOT—STARS

The blackness of the inside of my eyelids swirls with distraction. Eyes open or closed, my body refuses to sleep. I've listened to deep breath meditations through my headphones. I've worn myself out with pushups in the dark bedroom. Yet here I am, tossing and turning for the second night since I left Nickie at the hospital.

The woman, Nicole, transformed into Dr. Brader before she stepped out of the car. I watched her tuck away the raw emotion and build a barrier, brick by brick. We walked right through the lobby and into the one ER examining room. Joyce, ghostly pale but eyes open, lifted a hand to her granddaughter. Nickie's parents and Jeffrey were there, and at that point I was an unnecessary distraction in a suit. I texted Nathan for a ride home, gave Nickie's dad her car keys, and politely extracted myself from the family emergency.

It wasn't the place for a first date acquaintance.

Sunday before church, Diana got word that Joyce was back home and resting.

I startle awake again, sucking a gasp of air, as if I've stopped breathing. Since when does my body forget how to breathe when asleep? Kicking off the sheets, I whisper another prayer. "What? What's going on? I'm up. What am I missing?"

If thoughts of Nickie aren't circling, I'm analyzing what to do about work and Randy's promotion. Itching to call Emily, but refusing to let that situation ruin Christmas. Feet on the floor, I lean my elbows on my knees. "Lord, take it. Please, let me sleep." I gather handfuls of air around me as if plucking fruit from a tree and toss them over my head. "Take it."

It's an exercise I started years ago, literally casting my metaphorical burdens on Him.

I check my watch and groan. It's three fifteen, and it's been less than thirty minutes since I last looked at it. "Forget it," I mumble as I stand.

Dressed in my warmest clothes, and with Nathan's coveralls zipped to my chin, I sneak out of the house and stare at the bright snow. I breathe the fresh, cold air, enjoying the feel of it against my face. The wind has calmed into a gentle breeze. The blankets of snow on every surface reflect the lights of every holiday decoration, and it rivals any fantasyland imaginings.

The snow clouds have finally cleared, and I gaze at the vast expanse. Stars gleam against the black void. There's no light pollution in Hadley Springs, and the stars and moon really are the lights to govern the night. It's a clear enough sky that I can discern the Milky Way itself. I locate the Big Dipper then the Little Dipper and follow its handle to the

North Star. It's been too many years since I've been away from the city to be able to see them.

Praying as I walk, my boots make a pleasant crunch on the icy sidewalk. I speak softly, but the words fall from my tongue with intention. "Your timing is perfect. Your ways are perfect. Bless Nickie's family with your perfect plan for bringing Joyce and Jeffrey home to You. Please keep them together through the holidays. Don't let the enemy kidnap the joy of this season with death. You've conquered death. Your power is greater, and I know it's not beyond Your will to give us good things. Good memories. Good family holidays. Joyce and Jeffrey are good for Nickie. I know our bodies wear out and it will soon be time for them to sleep, but—"

I pause at an intersection, not sure if I'm waiting for the nonexistent traffic or inspiration on which way to turn. "But surround them with Your peace." I continue walking, knowing exactly where my steps are taking me.

Three minutes later Nickie's house appears across the street. Her car is parked in the driveway. All the lights are off and I walk on by, continuing my prayer. At the end of the block I cross the street, turn around and head back. Passing by her house the second time I look up and catch movement on the dark porch.

Nickie leans against the porch railing, wrapped in a red plaid blanket. "Hey."

"Hey." I stop, hands in my pockets.

There's a faint wisp of a cloud from her breath that catches the moonlight.

I hold my arms out in a show of peace. "This isn't what it looks like."

Her smile is clear in the snow-reflected light. "It looks

like you're walking around my neighborhood in the middle of the night."

"So." I laugh softly, relieved to see her again. "It's exactly what it looks like."

"I couldn't sleep either." She backs away from the railing to a wooden bench. "Come sit with me."

My boots are quiet on the snow-dusted porch steps. It's darker under the overhang of the roof. I sit beside her, our legs and arms brushing.

With no wind to whistle around the buildings or rattle branches, there's hardly any sound. A foreign land from what I've grown used to. No emergency sirens or traffic. No blaring TVs from neighboring hotel rooms. Nothing like my room in the city.

It's nice.

After a couple of minutes, I rest my arm around the back of the bench, and she leans her head against me.

It's really nice.

"How's Grandma Joyce?"

"She'll be fine." Nickie's shoulders lift and fall with a deep breath. "It's stupid really. I was too distracted over the past week and didn't monitor her diet and liquid intake. She was dehydrated, and it bottomed out her blood pressure."

"The text from your mom said she was unresponsive."

"When you're eighty-five, falling asleep in your recliner and not waking up is unresponsive. Cat-naps are normal, but this was—it was frightening. Grandpa's having a hard time about it. He wasn't with her that day either and blames himself, thinking he should have made sure she was drinking. They had an IV in her by the time I got to her."

"I'm sorry."

"It's my job to take care of them." Her voice sounds tired. "It's not Grandpa's fault. I was rushed and skipped her check-up, then slept all day, or was preening in the bath-room getting ready. It was one thing after another, but it can't happen again." She steadies her breath.

"You should be sleeping."

"Says my stalker."

"Aw, this does look bad, doesn't it?"

"If you were stalking, then I was lurking. I watched you trudge down the block and come back again. That might be worse."

"Skulking."

"That's not even a real word."

I lean over to pull my phone from my pocket, but she swats my arm.

"I believe you, Mr. Editor. You don't have to prove it."

Replacing my arm over her shoulders, I settle her against me.

She fits. "You weren't stalking, but you were thinking about me?"

I don't answer right away because I don't know what's happening. Obviously I was thinking about her. I could say yes. I could admit she hasn't left my thoughts since Saturday morning. I could say that I enjoyed our time together far more than I expected. Since we cleaned the slate in Diana's kitchen, talking with her, touching her, being next to her has been as easy as breathing. But to what end? I don't know which column to place her in my spreadsheet.

"I was hoping the fresh air would clear my head. Can't help it if my feet led me back to you."

"There's a line." She pokes a finger at my side through her blanket. "You get that from one of your books?"

"'All the world's a stage and all the men and women merely players.'"

"Shakespeare. At least give me a challenge, mister."

"'In vain have I struggled, it will not do—'"

"Jane Austen, I'm sure. Is that all you've got?"

"Dang, you are good."

"I'm a professional." Her voice shakes with a laugh.

"I edit the books, I don't write them. Let's see... 'Love each other as I have loved you.'"

She hums while thinking. "*Princess Bride?*"

"What? That's the Bible. Ha, I win."

The three bright stars of Orion's Belt are visible above the single ornamental tree in the neighbor's yard. The skeletal branches are white with a dusting of snow over a skin of ice.

"Mark?"

"Yeah?"

"Why doesn't this feel weird?"

I tighten my arm around her soft form. "That we're snuggled on your porch in the middle of the night?"

Her head against my shoulder nods a yes. I've been thinking the same thing, trying not to overanalyze every moment of our interactions, and failing. I like to plan. But I don't want to fix what isn't broken. This gives me hope that finding someone in Arizona to marry won't be as hard as I thought.

I've witnessed Cordy, even with her talk of kindred spirits and bosom friends, sabotage multiple relationships by overthinking. I didn't realize getting to know a woman could be this comfortable. Those awkward dates of my early twenties are proof I wasn't ready yet.

"When are you flying home?"

"Tomorrow. Which is good. There's important stuff I need to deal with at work."

"And then find a wife?" Her voice carries sarcasm, but I sense an honest question.

"That too." The quiet moments settle comfortably around us. As if the night and the chilled air and stars are enough without extra words.

My thoughts trail to our interrupted evening. Dr. Kendrick wasn't what I'd expected. When it counted, he didn't challenge my authority for getting Nickie to her family. He appeared truly concerned over the situation. I didn't note elements of jealousy as we worked together. "Tell me about Dr. Kendrick. What's your beef with him?"

"Oh, he's not so bad. Being a woman in my field, well, I think everyone should be careful in this profession, but I never want to make a patient or colleague uncomfortable or provide an opening for accusations or abuse. So I've always been careful with how I present myself at work."

Nickie lifts her head and stares across the street. "There's too much at stake. The things I see and hear and do. Physically, it's... I'm sure you can imagine. There's a huge level of trust involved. You wouldn't believe some of the nonsense I've dealt with from male patients. Most of it I handle, but I've transferred a couple patients to Preston. We need to be able to work well together, and my rule from the beginning was simply never to involve myself with people from work. Patients or otherwise. I know relationships between colleagues aren't uncommon, but there's been no sacrifice on my end. There's no spark with Preston."

I rub my hand along her arm, and she leans against me again.

"It's year after year of me trying to avoid his advances. He's friendly with everyone, but it's like the whole office is waiting for us to get together when I've never gone along with it. Now I get all worked up every time he texts. Like, why can't the guy leave me alone?"

"Sounds clear enough to me. I like to keep my personal life separate from work too. It seems odd he'd keep at it if you've made your stance known."

She readjusts her blanket and tucks her arms back inside her cocoon.

"You've told him clearly?"

"I've made it pretty clear, Mark. You'd think after avoiding him for so long he'd take the hint that I'm not—"

"No."

Nickie pulls away from my shoulder and faces me. "No?"

"Give me your phone. I want to read your convos."

"No."

I beckon with my gloved hand for her phone. "Words are my job. I can read your responses, analyze how it could be interpreted, and we can see if you've been as clear as you think."

"I will not give you my phone."

"Okay." I shrug. "Say that to Preston, 'I will not engage in romantic relationships with colleagues.' If you've set the standard and he keeps coming around, then we have a problem."

"We?"

"You have a problem."

"Mark, what are we?"

I take my time to think. She's not a silly girl to be hurt by the truth, especially when there's not much between us in the first place. How could there be? It's been mere days. If we were in a different place at a different time, maybe we could pursue something else. As it stands, a fun date—half of a date—is all it was. Yet I can't ignore the rightness of how this feels. "I'd like to be your friend."

"Friends who shared a kiss?"

"You don't make it easy, you know that?"

She looks at me with that calm, sweet expression. "It was fun for a night."

If we were more than friends it would be a simple thing to close the gap between us. To press my lips against her forehead. The natural progression would be wrapping both arms around her. She'd probably drop the blanket in favor of threading her fingers into my hair.

Scenes from recent manuscripts flit through my brain and I want to try them out. To sit her on the porch railing and lean into a slow kiss. Instead I smile and tear my gaze away. "Best night of the whole year."

"Thanks for making me feel special. I'd like to be friends. Can I—" A whoosh of an exhale cuts off her words. She slowly stands, the blanket draping just past her knees. "I'd like to spend more time with you before you go. Can I drive you to the airport at least?"

"I have an evening flight. So we don't need to leave until about six."

She reaches her hands toward me, and I offer mine. She tugs me to my feet then wraps us both in her blanket. "I think you're wrong about it not being easy."

"Is that so?"

"It's too easy that I don't want to let you go." Her arms pull me into a hug that feels like home.

Being her friend is easy. Pretending I don't remember what it feels like to have Nicole Brader's warm lips against mine is the hard part. If I had known friendship could be like this... but every second I stand here wrapped in her embrace makes me want to figure out how to stay. As if there wasn't a career crisis waiting for me back home.

I don't believe the lie that I must rewrite my whole life to force a situation that isn't meant to be. I've edited too many grand gestures of the man speeding toward the airport with the false assumption that if he doesn't catch her in the next two minutes she'll be gone forever. As if God gives us one tiny chance at happiness to be blown away if we don't jump at the exact right moment. He won't let me get to the end of the book having missed a tiny footnote: See wife, page one.

I've committed my work and schedule to the Lord. He'll establish my plans. Halfway back to Diana's house, my feet still protest they're going the wrong way. I pump my arms and move into a slow jog to erase Nicole's lingering warmth.

*Project: Find a Wife* has its merits. I believe it's the right plan of action for me to pursue at this time. With that hope on the horizon, returning to work and my regular routine will make this holiday in Hadley Springs a pleasant memory that is sure to pale when I meet the woman God has planned for me.

# 13

## NICKIE

### TUESDAY, DECEMBER 26

CAMELOT SOUNDTRACK—WHAT DO THE SIMPLE FOLK DO?

Chaos dances around me in the forms of red-headed twins, a blond toddler, and a weeping pre-teen as we load Mark into the car. The man travels light with nothing but a backpack. The driveway turned to slush in the afternoon sun and the ruts are beginning to re-freeze. The short winter days have left us in the dark again and the porch light illuminates the front sidewalk where he's been caught.

"Hey, hey, hey." Mark soothes Lauren, crouching in front of her. His palms cup her face as he thumbs her tears away. "I'm gonna miss you too, okay? Have your mom call me whenever you want to chat."

"I—" Lauren hiccups through the emotion. "I just—" She gives up and throws herself in Mark's embrace. "I just feel like you're the only one who understands." I catch his gaze over Lauren's shoulder with a sad smile. These kids really love him.

Diana tugs Lauren into a hug to release her cousin. "Goodbye, Mark. Give us a call when you land."

High-fives, more hugs, a kiss for the baby, another round of high-fives, and Mark is finally in the passenger seat, window rolled down waving goodbye. The kids sprint down the sidewalk in their sweatpants and T-shirts until they reach the intersection.

Mark collapses into the seat, eyes closed, with his finger on the window button. "Whew. I'm exhausted." His eyes drift open, and he smiles. "Hey, beautiful. How was the rest of your Christmas?"

Oh boy. I could get used to this. Warmth expands from my chest to fingertips on the steering wheel. I wasn't lying all those years I claimed I didn't need a man—but I'd never met this man. How does one know they don't need caramel cheesecake if they've never tasted it? Nobody needs cheese-cake everyday, especially not the whole thing. A slice every now and then is good for the soul. Mark could be my cheesecake.

He's still looking at me with a gentle smile, waiting for my answer.

"Christmas was fine, thank you very much." I pop on the overhead light and shake my wrist in Mark's face while I concentrate on driving. "Look at my fancy new sparkles."

His hands adjust the cuff of my blue sweatshirt to expose a diamond tennis bracelet. He makes the proper hum of appreciation with a murmured, "Very nice."

"Grandma passed it on to me. Jeffrey got this for her on their thirtieth anniversary."

Mark seems to be taking an extended look at the jewelry, and I savor the warmth of his hands. His thumb slides under the bracelet along the inside of my wrist, and I hide a shiver by taking my arm back. I reach overhead to fumble for the light, but he intercepts my hand.

"Wait, what's this one?" He examines my ring, a gold band on my ring finger studded with a line of rubies.

"Joyce got this one from her dad for her sweet sixteen. It pays to be the only granddaughter."

He slips it off my finger and holds it to the light. "What does your mom think about being skipped over?"

"She's got her share. Dad got her a bracelet like this last year, but I think hers is cubic zirconium. This one's real. Besides, Mom and I have borrowed Grandma's and each other's jewelry interchangeably since I was old enough to be trusted. It is fun to have my own though. To wear them with a sweatshirt and feel like a queen."

He doesn't say anything and a trickle of insecurity drips on me, as if my courage has faltered at the threat of a storm. "Am I talking too much? Sorry. How was your Christmas? Now I feel bad. Should I have let CJ or Diana drive you? The kids could have spent some extra time with you." I reach into the cupholder for a pack of gum and offer it to him. "Gum?"

"No thanks." Mark returns my ring then unbuckles and wriggles around in his seat as he takes off his neon ski jacket. "There is no CJ. Stop calling her that. Cordy got a boyfriend for Christmas. I guess she and Gilbert—"

A squeal bursts from my mouth as I shove in a piece of gum, and Mark's whole body spasms in panic. "What is it?"

"Sorry! I'm just happy for them."

"Well, can you—" He gestures to the road. "Can you not do that while you're driving? You're making me nervous."

"Yeah. Sorry. But I totally called it." The taillights of a Suburban bounce in front of us as we merge onto the highway. A green sign comes into view: Omaha 92 miles.

We spend a good amount of time swapping stories

about our family Christmas traditions and get-togethers then swing back to the Cordy and Gilbert development.

Mark pops open the glove box and finds a case of my old soundtrack CDs. "You know Gilbert pretty well?" He flips through until finding one he approves of and slides it into the player. I'd tell him the speakers are broken, but he'll figure it out sooner or later, the snoop.

"Oh yeah. He's my brother's best friend, and we all went to school together. He and I actually tried going out once. It was weird as all-get-out. He held my hand at prom." I make a face at the memory. "I know he was just trying to be nice, like that's what we were supposed to do, but it was so awkward. Super-duper awkward. Definitely no spark there. But worth a try I guess."

He pushes a few buttons, ejects the CD and puts it back in. "What is it with you girls and giving things a try?" Mark doesn't seem the least bit frustrated as he ejects the CD a second time, then angles it to the light to check for scratches.

"Sometimes you don't know until you know... you know?"

He pauses his examination and leans dangerously close to me. "I always know," he says in a stage whisper. The clean smell of him fills my head, and I'm momentarily distracted. I don't know if it's his soap, detergent, or deodorant—maybe just *Essence of Mark*, but I kind of, definitely, for sure love it. Love it more than cheesecake.

"Oh my lanta." I keep talking because I'm in trouble here if I don't. "You're full of it. You're telling me you've never gone out with someone and it fell flat?"

"Absolutely." The CD is returned to the case, and he pulls out another one. "But there's a mutual understanding —" He pushes a few buttons on the broken stereo. "—that a first date doesn't guarantee a second date. That's the point of dating. I'm not making out with every girl I date. And I'm definitely not about to hold someone's hand or kiss a girl to *try it out* with them."

"You held my hand."

He aggressively twists the knobs and *click, click, clicks* different buttons. I'm not sure if he's irritated with this conversation or the stereo. "I held your hand because I wanted to, and it wasn't awkward."

"How do you know it wasn't awkward for me? What if you wanted to hold my hand, but I didn't want to hold your hand?"

"That's what I'm saying! I wasn't trying it out. I wouldn't have touched you if I wasn't sure." He sounds exasperated now, and I bite my lower lip to keep from laughing. "We'd already kissed at the door, and you seemed to enjoy that just fine."

"How do you *know*?" I steal a glance at his face. Mindless chatter between adults who went on a date but aren't a couple. Definitely not a couple because I'm literally driving him to the airport before any chance of a second date.

"Nickie, you're making this way too complicated. If a girl doesn't want to hold hands, I sure as heck won't reach over and grab her."

"Hmmm. I don't know about you, mister. You're starting to sound like an uppity Know-It-All."

"Quit your fussing, She-Goose. We both know you liked it. There were signs. You reciprocated. Do you need a recap? You leaned into me to get away from Christy, you grabbed *my* hand at the registration table, and you confessed, with words, about how you wanted me to kiss you again. Now tell me why can't I get this CD to play."

I ignore his question for another two miles while he

continues to fiddle with the machine. "Calm down over there. Why you so fidgety?"

He slumps into the seat, unbuckles his seatbelt, stretches his arms all the way to the windshield and then rebuckles. "I'm a little claustrophobic. It's fine. I'll take a pill before I get on the plane. But really, what's wrong with this CD?"

"What'd you pick?"

"*Camelot.*"

"That's my favorite." I sigh, so-sad-too-bad. "The speaker's broken. I can sing if you're bored already."

Mark snorts a laugh and mutters something too soft for me to hear while closing the glove box. "Take it away, *prima donna.*"

*And then* he rests his elbow on the center console, hand palm up. The backs of his fingers brush the side of my leg, daring me to take it. I glance from his hand back to the road, heart thudding at the casual offer of intimacy. Taunting what *he knows.*

I've spent years with a firm shield in place for important reasons that evade me at the moment. I've never needed a man, although right now I rather like the idea of this one.

I don't need one, perhaps I want one. I want *him.* I want Mark. Even with his laughable plans for his presumptive wife project. I like this one. He's honest. There's no second-guessing his motives or wondering what he's thinking. And the same impulsivity that had me inviting him to a gala is warring within me now to take his hand. Go for it. After all, I started this. No pressure.

I'm so close to saying yes.

I already know how comfortable it is there. It would be easy. So simple. So—so risky.

While I'm debating, headlights reflect against the sign:

Omaha 40 miles. A pin deflates my dreams as I'm reminded that long-distance romance is no romance at all. Friends don't ride around in cars holding hands.

Mark's finger twitches while he's straight-faced with the barest hint of a smile tugging the corner of his lips. "What'll it be?" He's asking about the music, but implying much more.

"Thanks." I quickly spit out my gum and smoosh it onto his waiting palm. "I could probably do the whole *Camelot* score from memory. I'll play Guinevere, you take Arthur?" At this point my attempt at playing it cool dissolves into laughter as he stares at his hand in disgust. "No? How about *Hairspray*?"

"Better than a fish, I guess," he says while using an old wrapper to take care of the gum.

There's little traffic, yet I maintain a healthy distance between us and the red lights far in front. I keep my gaze on the road and launch into the trumpet's intro of "You Can't Stop the Beat" from *Hairspray*. "Bada bum bum, bum, bum, bada, bum... Bum bum! Come on, Mark, snap your fingers or something."

A vehicle tails us obnoxiously close and the LED lights that should be illegal blind me from both the rearview and side mirror at the same time. "Ack, have a heart, man," I mutter. He attempts to pass, but decides against it as an oncoming semi bears down in the other lane.

I slow below the speed limit and hug the shoulder as close as I can. "Go for it, buddy. But you're being an idiot." My fingers tingle with the spike of adrenaline as the guy rides my tail.

"What's his deal?" Mark turns to look behind us. "He's way too close."

It's a black pickup that swerves around us the moment

the incoming lane clears. Ahead, he speeds into a curve in the road then loses control and spins a complete circle that blocks both lanes of traffic. I pump the brake, knowing it will do little to stop the impending collision.

Wet road.

Black ice.

Nothing I can do.

"Nickie!" Mark flattens against his seat.

"Hold on." My voice is foreign to my ears. I jerk the steering wheel to the right, hoping to land us in the ditch instead of a full-on T-bone.

My wheels spin on the same invisible ice. "God, help!"

The diamonds of my bracelet flash before my eyes as I wrap both arms over my head to brace for impact.

A scream. Mine?

A catastrophic crunch as we smash the bed of the truck.

I'm weightless as we flip into the ditch. My body jerks in too many directions. I try to shield my head in my arms as we're tossed from the road. Inertia slams my head against the window. Glass cracks against my skull and the world turns black.

## 14

# MARK

I'm walking away from an upside-down car. Which is strange because a second ago there were headlights in my eyes from a truck spinning in front of us. Nickie's scream and then—Oh, there it is. A dozen feet away I stop, hands on hips, and examine the pickup truck. It's parked on the shoulder with a large dent on the side of the bed.

A man in jeans and a canvas coat stumbles out of the driver's seat. He's unsteady but manages to stay on his feet as he runs past me. "Oh, God. Oh, God. Oh, God." He says a few other words that I wouldn't put in the same sentence with our Creator.

I feel a tugging to keep moving away from the accident, but I'm concerned for Nickie. Where is she? I turn a slow circle and wonder if she's still in the car. I follow the man. The exposed undercarriage of Nickie's car fogs in the cold. There's a lot of whistling like steam escaping from a broken tube. I don't know anything about cars, but it's not good.

The man is on his knees by the front window, hand

pressing a phone to his ear. "Hello? I need to report an accident on ninety-two. We need an ambulance right away. Oh my God, um, yeah, I'm fine, but they're upside down." He wipes his nose and runs around to the other side. He lets out a few more choice words. "We're just west of Wahoo... I don't know! No, past Brainard. What do I do? Should I— Oh God—Yeah, I'm safe, we're, um, off the road... It's bad... Gary. Uh—Gary Brindle. My name's Gary."

I look at my feet in the snow. Huh. How did I get out of the car? I take another step toward the vehicle and a wave of immense peace and love washes over me that halts my steps. It's so strong I'm surprised that I can't physically see the emotion. It's like nothing I've ever experienced.

A man in jeans and an old fashioned striped polo stands beside me. He has my brown eyes and thick brown hair though it's cut in a distinctly longer style. He's incredibly familiar. Like family. I tilt my head, taking in his peaceful face. He's—

"Granddad?"

"I've been waiting for you, Mark." He pulls me into a hug.

Happiness like I've never felt bursts around me like Fourth of July sparklers, and I'm laughing. "Granddad! What are you doing here?"

His embrace is full of strength, and I clutch him against me. He smells of my childhood. There's no name for it except the embodiment of comfort and safety that creates a pang of longing in my chest.

I'm filled with this deep current of love although something's still not right. Granddad looks like the photos in Mom's old scrapbooks. Younger than I'd known him. I press my hands against the sides of his face, and he lets me turn his head from side to side. He's solid.

Memories flit like an Instagram reel, faster and faster as I absorb images of my life from my earliest memories until moments ago when... I spin to look at the car. "Nickie?"

The man from the truck is sitting in the dirty snow with his head between his knees, shoulders shaking.

"Am I dead?" I pat myself down noting the smoothness of my black T-shirt, the empty pockets of my track pants. I'm solid. I breathe in the air. I note the sharp chill in my lungs, but I also recognize that I no longer need it.

Granddad's hand on my shoulder pulls my attention from the crash. "You're more alive right now than you've ever been."

It occurs to me that I'm not in pain. I'm not scared. Underneath everything I see, smell, feel, and hear there's an overwhelming sense of *not yet*. I move one foot closer to the car, with a hand still on Granddad's arm, worried if I break contact he'll disappear. How did I get out of the car and not Nickie? Is she still trapped inside?

"You need to stay," Granddad says. The timbre of his voice is just as I remember it.

The reality of what's happening slices into my previous joy, and I pull him against me, burying my face into his neck. I'm not embarrassed by the tears and audible sobs. "I've missed you so much. I want to come with you."

"I know," he answers, holding me tight. "It's going to be okay, but you have work yet to do here. He says it's not your time." Granddad kisses my forehead like he used to do when I was five. Then he chuckles, the sound a beautiful ache of a forgotten memory. "You and God have plans, remember?"

I wipe my eyes on the back of my forearms. "Will I see you again?"

"Eventually." He holds me upright. "We have a place reserved for you at the table. You're gonna love—"

"Mark! Wake up!" Nickie's panicked voice invades my thoughts.

I turn my head, but it's hard because I'm hanging upside down, buckled into the car.

"You're awake. You're a—" Her voice cuts out with a ragged intake of breath. Her blond hair pools on the roof of the car, and there's a dark stain along the opposite side of her head.

"It's gonna be okay." I answer automatically. "Help is coming." I scratch at my seatbelt and look over at Nickie as I hear her hyperventilating. "Hey, hey, hey. Breathe. Keep breathing. Baby, stay with me. Look at me. You're okay."

"I'm not— I'm not okay. This isn't okay. I'm not— You weren't breathing. Mark, you weren't breathing. I can't— God, it hurts. I need—" Her breaths are coming too fast and shallow.

I quit fighting my seatbelt and put my hand on her shoulder. "Dr. Brader, you need to focus."

"Don't leave me."

"I'm not leaving you."

15

———

CORDY

Gilbert hums a line from an upbeat tune he's been toying with all day for his latest composition, and I repeat the notes back to him with words, "Cheetos, banditos, and smeetos with me. Lalalala." I pause my interpretive dance in my lovely cottage kitchen and wait for his applause at my superior writing skills.

He quirks an eyebrow from where he sits at the round table then returns to his scritch-scratching in his notebook.

I bow a number of times and sweep off my imaginary top hat like a circus ring master, and then clap for myself. "Bravo! Wonderful! Yay!" Because Gilbert is the cutest when he's pretending to ignore me—as if I'll simply stop being ridiculous from his mature example—I continue clapping, adding in a stomp here and there. I snap my fingers in rhythm and sing the line again. "Cheetos, banditos, and smeetos with me! Lalalalaaaaa."

I dance my way closer and closer until I'm near enough to knock my hip into his side. *Bop... Bop... Bop...*

By the third time my hip jostles him while he's trying to write, a laugh mixed with a baby growl is my warning before he comes for me. Pencil dropped, he snakes an arm around my waist so fast I couldn't pull away if I tried—which I obviously did not. As I squeal, he pulls me onto his lap and nuzzles his face into my neck. The touch is heady, and the air exits my lungs like the soft breeze through spring flowers.

His kisses both paralyze and excite me. Gilbert brushes my mane of hair out of his way and leaves his hand cradling the side of my face. "What do you want?"

"I have nobody for to play with." I pout like Lisa when she's lonely.

"You're the most needy girlfriend I've ever had."

I smoosh his face between my hands, his week's worth of a full beard scratching my palms. "The best, you mean. The best girlfriend ever in the history of forever." Happiness seeps from me in laughter. My cheeks hurt from all the smiling this Christmas. *Girlfriend!* I've held the title for a day and a half, and I'm not over it. I'm Gilbert's girlfriend. The luckiest girl in the whole wide world.

He pecks a kiss on the tip of my nose. "In the history of forever."

My phone buzzes in my back pocket against Gilbert's lap. "Woo!" He yelps and dumps me on the floor.

It's an unknown number, and I decline the call while laughing. "Guess I should find a new place for my phone if you're going to overreact about everything."

An immediate text comes through.

> Unknown: I'm with Mark Brader, please answer if you can.

"Hang on, this is weird. Look at this." I stand while turning the screen to Gilbert. "What does that mean?"

"Isn't Mark on a plane?"

"Soon, but I don't think it was—Ope, he's calling again. Hello?"

"Cordy?" It's Mark's voice but weak. Scared. Different than I've ever heard it. The siren of an ambulance wails in the background. "I'm okay. But, um, do you have a minute?"

"Of course! Mark. What's going on?"

"Well, we were driving and there was—" He gasps for air as if he can't get enough. "—there was this—we were in a wreck and Nickie's—um—Cordy, are you there?"

"Yeah, I'm here." I switch to speakerphone and ease into the chair next to Gilbert. "Where are you?" I ask with a calm assurance that I don't feel. "Are you safe?"

"I'm in an ambulance. I'm okay. It's bad, but she's alive. Was talking. Nothing seemed broken. She hit her head. The guy says she's stable, but I'm strapped to this board. I need—I can't get enough air."

In all the years of my life with Mark—cousin, best friend, advisor—he's never needed me like this. "Mark, you're safe now. Can you—"

"Hi, this is David. I'm the paramedic with Mark." The familiarity of the voice is confusing. "Mark wanted me to let you know that he's okay. We're taking him to—"

"David K. the home inspector?" I glance at Gilbert and mouth *What?* David and I met for a date last week in Omaha after my failed experiment with online dating.

"Yeah, hi. Also a paramedic. Not the best way to hear from me again."

"Wow, weird. Listen, David, Mark's incredibly claustrophobic."

"Gotcha. That would explain some things."

"Does he have to be on the board?"

"Yes, he does."

"But it sounds like he's hyperventilating."

"Yep. But we need to protect him from spinal injury until we get X-rays. The woman with him is in the other bus. She's stable. We're taking them both to CHI Health. They were in a rollover, and we didn't locate their phones. Can you contact her family? Hang on." There's rustling and low talking on the other end.

The pressure of Gilbert's hand on my shoulder releases, and I watch him pull out his phone and make a call.

"David? I have someone here with me who's calling her family."

"Great. If they're coming from outside Omaha, please ask them not to come to the hospital at this time. We've had every crew out on call tonight. The roads are not safe. We'll know more in an hour."

Gilbert nods that he's heard and backs away into the bedroom.

"I'm putting the phone to Mark's ear. Can you talk to him? Try to calm him down?"

"Cordy?" Mark's breathless voice is a knife to my heart, and I would do anything to help him.

"Hey Mark, you're doing so well! Look at you not dying. Bravo!" I force a cheerful lilt to my voice.

"Ugh, Cordy, you're—the worst."

"Yet you called me because you love me the most," I brag.

"You're the only—number I—have memorized."

"Breathe slower, please. You're panting into the phone, and it's obnoxious." I hope my attempts at humor will distract him enough to get through this. "Slow down. Here, do it with me. In, in, in, in, out, out, out, out. You're terrible at this game! Can I have your old CD collection if you don't make it?"

His shallow breaths change into either shallow laughs or sobs. "Too soon, Cordy. I think— You're gonna—" He stops talking to pant a few more breaths. "Can you tell him to let me off of this?"

"You're gonna make it, Mark. Close your eyes for me, okay? Close your eyes and think of yesterday. We were sitting around the tree singing carols with Frank Sinatra, and Lisa was asleep in your lap. Wasn't that the sweetest feeling? Remember when her eyes finally gave up the fight and drifted closed? She was so precious. Think about how she felt in your arms with her head resting against your chest."

Gilbert returns, tucking his phone away. He moves his chair closer and sits with his arms wrapped around me.

"Mark, you're doing great. Keep your eyes closed." I cling to Gilbert's arm at my waist and wipe the tear from my face. I hope I can control the tone of my voice even as emotion leaks through my eyes. "You're sitting on the couch with Lisa asleep and the twins wrestling on the carpet. You're completely safe."

"I'm going to be late for work tomorrow."

"Heck yes, you are! Best excuse ever."

"I've never been late for work."

"Guess you'll finally get to use a few of your sick days."

"I need unstrapped. Tell him to let me out." The fear in his voice is too much.

I dip my head forward and tighten my hold on Gilbert. "Dear God, watch over Mark and Nickie and the doctors, nurses, drivers, paramedics and bring them safely through this."

"Hey, it's David. I'm going to hang up now. We're approaching the bay. Again, please don't try to come tonight. I'll give your number to the desk and someone will call when we have updates, and go ahead text me his parents' number or anyone else you think he'd like to talk to. He should be free to make some calls in about an hour. Dispatch will send someone to bring their phones if they find them."

"Okay, bye." I stare at the silent phone at the table.

Gilbert untangles himself. "Did you really ask for Mark's CD collection?"

I hide my face on my arms at the table. "I was trying to make him laugh. Lands to the living, Gilbert. I need to call my aunt and uncle. Will you get the address to the hospital? David says we shouldn't come up. But we need to call everyone—"

Gilbert holds my coat open. "Come on, babe. I'm taking you to Diana's. You can make some calls on the way."

I slip my arms into the purple coat. "Thank you, Gilbert. I'm so glad you're here."

He presses a kiss to my forehead. "Me too."

16

———

NICKIE

WEDNESDAY, DECEMBER 27

THE GREATEST SHOWMAN SOUNDTRACK—TIGHTROPE

The sustained beep of the EKG monitor drags me into full consciousness. My eyes open to a dimly lit room. That noise is bad. Someone's flat-lined. Who? Where?

I turn my head, and pain slams through my neck and into my skull.

A heavyset woman in blue scrubs enters with concern in her eyes. When she catches my gaze, she smiles. "You're awake." She shuts off the terrible sound then lifts the blanket off my chest. "You've pulled off your sticker again."

A loose hospital gown barely covers my essentials, and I find the lead line grasped in my fist. "Sorry," I scratch out the word, throat burning.

"How you feeling, honey?" She takes the cord and reattaches it under my left breast. "Your husband just stepped out."

I blink in confusion. "Mark?"

"Hasn't left your side except in search of coffee."

"He's okay?"

"Right as rain after we let him off the gurney. You're the one we've been praying for. Took a hit on your head. Try not to move too much. Can you tell me how you feel?"

"It hurts."

"Where does it hurt? On a scale of one to ten?"

I close my eyes and track my body. Toes wiggle. That's fine. Fingers flex. I lift my right knee and gasp as the pain zings my spine. "Back. Neck. Head. It's a ten when I move. But we can chart at seven. I suppose it could get worse. You never know until you know..." My voice trails off, and I suddenly want to see Mark with all the energy left in me. "Any fractures?"

"Nothing broken. We ran a CT scan of your head and spine, but aside from the bruising and the cut on the head, you're unscathed. You'll be in pain from the whiplash. Concussion of course."

I'd love to see those scans myself. "Why was I asleep?"

"It's the middle of the night. You're tired."

I read her nametag. "Carol, tell me the truth."

"Oh, honey. Sometimes the body protects us from things we don't need to remember. You've got a cut on the side of your head with a few sutures, and your entire body will be sore from the impact." Carol places a hand on my shoulder as if to stall the questions she knows are simmering. "Dr. Gyle will be back in the morning to answer any questions. The best you can do is try to sleep as much as you can. Can you tell me what you remember?"

"Um, I was driving. There was a truck that passed me. It was going too fast." I tap my finger against the tan blanket and stare at the speckled drop panel ceiling. That's all there is. "Mark is here? He's missed his flight."

"I tried to talk him into getting a hotel for a good night's rest, but he wouldn't budge from that chair." She pats my shin over the blanket. "Sure is nice to be loved. Can you tell me your birthday?" Carol pulls the mobile computer cart in from the hallway. "And your social?"

I rattle off the numbers, and she nods while looking at the screen.

"Can I have some water, please?"

"You're awake!" Mark's raspy voice pulls my attention to the doorway. His silhouette is framed against the brighter lights of the hallway a moment before he moves into the room. His gait is different, as if he's favoring his right leg.

I grip the blanket against my chest, embarrassed to be lying here, hooked up to too many cords and wearing next to nothing. The machine beside me beeps a warning—my heart rate has spiked.

Carol types something on the computer and says, "I'll be back in a couple minutes with some water."

"We've got to bust out of here." Mark hovers over me. "The coffee is atrocious." He gently trails his fingers over my forehead. The sensation is like a tranquilizer shot that immediately banishes the tension from my face and neck. "Oh, Nickie, it's good to see you awake."

"Your leg?"

"Bruised my kneecap. Whiplash, etc. I'm fine. How're you?" He's wearing black scrubs that are too big for him.

"Did you tell her we were married?"

"I told her my name and didn't correct her assumption in case this was going to be an immediate-family-only situation. They'll figure it out."

"Hmm." We seem to be allowing that assumption a lot lately. "What happened to your clothes?"

"I upgraded." Mark steps back looking over his outfit as if seeing it for the first time, the styrofoam cup held out in one hand. "What do you think? Could I pass as your nurse?"

I smile, careful not to move my head too much. "Nurse Brader, I'm noticing acute onset tachycardia and mild respiratory distress. Can you monitor her oxygen saturation and let me know if there's further decline?"

"Dr. Brader, I have no idea what you said, but our patient's apparent suffering seems triggered by proximity to an exceptionally good-looking nurse."

"What do you recommend, Nurse Brader?"

"Continued observation."

"You're sweet." I point to the chair by the bed. "Will you sit for a while? I should probably call my parents."

"It's three in the morning. I talked with them last around midnight. They'll come up this afternoon when the sun's out and bring you home."

"What about you?"

"I've another flight scheduled in a few hours. Already have a car booked."

"So soon?"

He nods, staring at the empty cup crushed between two hands.

"But your stuff. Isn't it trapped in the car?"

"Someone in a uniform came by an hour ago. They found our phones and my backpack." He nods to the corner of the room. "I've got to get home before Randy takes it all."

"Who's Randy?"

"Did I tell you about New York?"

I start to shake my head but catch the movement in time and say, "No. What about New York?"

"A promotion I'm expecting before the end of the year. You know what, forget New York." Mark walks to the door. "I can't believe I'm doing this." He turns, pauses with hands on hips like a hero with too much weight on his shoulders, then limps back to my bedside. "Would you give up everything and everyone and move across the country for someone? For a husband?"

A whole lot of nothing stuffs my brain. My skull is filled with cotton gauze soaking up thoughts as they form. I sift through the data and try to diagnose this conversation. My dry mouth tries to swallow, and I gently cough, trying not to strain my overwrought muscles.

"Of course not. Why would you?" Mark folds the rim of his styrofoam cup all the way around until it breaks off in a single ring. "I enjoyed spending time with you. If things were different. If you weren't here, and I didn't have everything established in Phoenix, I could see us together. More than friends. Things being as they are... I'm going home. I've got it all written out, and I've dedicated this year to finding a wife. I want to get married. Start a family. The whole thing."

"Sounds like you have it all planned." The voice is mine, but it feels like someone else speaking. It's a terrible plan written by a man too scared to take a chance outside of his curated control. Whiplash. This is what emotional whiplash feels like. "Mark, this feels like you're breaking up with me when we were never a couple." He's running away without giving us a chance.

"I have some ideas that would help you around the house with your grandparents." He carries on, refusing to acknowledge the possibility of *us*. "Some spreadsheets and reminders. A meal delivery service. You can hire a crew for the snow. Just because you're the main caretaker doesn't mean a CNA or someone can't come in once a day and help. If you want I can run the numbers and—"

"Mark, I'm really tired," I say gently. "Can we talk about this in the morning?"

"Yeah, of course. Sorry. I wanted to fix something." He stands and tosses the cup into the trash. "I'm going to borrow your shower. Goodnight. I'll just..."

I slowly turn my face away and let the weight of my eyelids shut out the world. I listen to the slow intake and release of each breath and try to sink back into oblivion and away from the pain pulsing through my body. I hear the low thread of his backpack zipper then the click of the bathroom door. Rustle of clothes. Spray of water. His toothbrush clinks against the side of the sink. The metal loops on the shower curtain rattle against the rod as it's opened and closed.

A tear burns a trail across my temple, and I hate that it's there. I hate that it betrays me. I knew Mark was leaving. We were never a *we*.

Just because he's funny and handsome. An amazing uncle and stupidly responsible. And that tattoo I still know nothing about. There is absolutely, one hundred percent, no reason to feel like half of my heart has been amputated because a man, who randomly chose my favorite CD, walked away.

I've been independently content for thirty-two years. But it doesn't feel like independence to let him go. It feels like surrendering contentment I've just discovered.

17

———

MARK

I've heard of the nightmare before Christmas, but I'm living the nightmare before New Year's. Even though I'm back at work in time for our weekly department meeting, my world is still spinning off its axis. The accident, the hospital, the flight—too much has happened for it to still be Wednesday.

Hi, I'm Mark Brader. I have my life together. I'm never late for work. I rarely take a sick day. I've never turned in a project late. I've never been passed over for a promotion that I've earned.

I don't second-guess my choices. I make plans and follow through. I know what I want from life and relentlessly pursue it.

Until today.

Until Nickie.

*God, why did you tease me with that attraction?* I sit at the dark hardwood conference table next to my assistant, Emily, and try to care about what she's explaining. Something about an unscheduled meeting last night. It's hard to care about anything right now. Maybe it's the lingering effect of the anxiety pill from this morning so I could fly without my claustrophobia taking over. My pen drags across the side column of my notebook. I lift it in a series of dashes across the bottom edge of the page and slowly outline an X in the corner before I add a shadowed edge for a three-dimensional shape that pops off the page.

Ho-hum. I'm a doodler now while thinking of a woman halfway across the country who has too many things to worry about to add me to the list.

Awesome.

I press the heel of my hand against my eyebrow and the flex sends an ache through my shoulder that an extra-strength ibuprofen doesn't curtail.

"Cute." Emily taps the page with the metal stylus from her tablet. "X marks the spot. You got treasure buried somewhere?"

"Yep." Treasure walking around in snowy Nebraska. Argh. No. The medicine is messing with me, I should be excited for next week after I get to talk to some of the guys from church. Someone is bound to have the name of at least one female recommendation.

"I really am sorry, Mark. I don't understand why you're not the one going to New York. I know how much we've worked for this, you've worked for this."

We're the only two in the room, yet she lowers her voice. "Randy is great, but he confided in me this morning that even he's confused. It should be you!"

"It's done. Let's not talk about it." The tired reply rumbles through the gravel in my throat. My pen has a mind of its own as the dashed line grows into a two lane highway on the page. New York, New Shmork. I don't even care.

That dream fizzled when it was swiped from my grip. Besides, if I'm focused on building a family, New York would have made things difficult. May as well stay here in the valley where I have better connections. We'll get this meeting over with, congratulate everyone. Yada-yada. Move forward with *Project: Find a Wife*.

Cold fingers brush the side of my face, and I jerk away from Emily's touch. "Sorry," she whispers. "You've got a bruise on your face. It looks like it really hurts. Your email said there was a delayed flight. Did something happen?"

"We got in a wreck on the way to the airport."

She makes a noise like she's seen a gross spider. When I turn my head, with effort, she's pressing her fingers against her mouth. "Are you—" She lowers her hands. "Are you okay?"

I lift both hands from the table in a *What does it look like?* gesture. "Obviously."

She'd probably pass out completely if I told her I think I might have died, just for a minute, but if I tell anyone about that, it won't be Emily. I'm not even sure what that was, probably a dream, and I sure won't be telling people I'm seeing things.

More and more the past few months, Emily's been wedging her way into my personal life. It feels intentional. I'll need to have a talk with her about that next week.

When she first started working for us, I loved her efficiency and the way she seemed to know what I needed before I even asked. She's still great, but she's changed. She lingers now until I dismiss her. I don't know how else to describe it. Could be that she's too efficient and getting bored. I'll have to see if Randy has noticed the shift. We could have her clean out the supply closets or something.

"Why didn't you say that? A delayed flight, Mark? Really? You could have died! This is why I hate Nebraska."

"Have you ever been to Nebraska?"

"Ew, never. Why would I? You shouldn't go there anymore either, especially during the winter."

"My family is there."

"Make them come here. This is a much better place."

And ironically, I would have agreed with her until recently.

"You should go home. Let me drive you home."

"I'll go home after the meeting."

She scoffs. "They already postponed the meeting from this morning until now, so that you could be here. Mrs. Emmerson could have waited until tomorrow. Or next week. You're not a machine."

The warning beat of approaching high heels snaps Emily's posture straight. I click and reclick the end of my pen as Mrs. Emmerson sweeps into view, dressed in a navy pencil skirt and crisp white blouse, with the matching jacket unbuttoned down the front. "Of course he's not a machine. That's why we love him. If machines could do what Mr. Brader does for us, we'd have no use for him. Just as we have no use for assistants who run their mouths. Emily, please find Mr. Chavez. I'd like to start on time."

I flick my gaze to the wall-mounted clock. Three minutes to four. Emily and I were eight minutes early. Randy still has three minutes to spare.

Even though I hired and onboarded Emily two years ago, she works for the whole editorial department at Lakeview Publishing—Mrs. Emmerson, who's CEO and Editor in Chief, then Randy Chavez and me as acquiring editors, and our line editor who only works remote. Emily is also a scheduling go-between for the production team, design, marketing, etc.

"How was your holiday, Mr. Brader?" Pausing from pulling out the seat at the head of the table, fine lines appear around Mrs. Emmerson's eyes as she studies me. "You don't look yourself. Are you feeling under the weather?"

"Why was I passed over for the promotion?"

"Because I need you here."

"Why?"

"Let's wait until the team is seated, shall we?"

"I'd rather not."

Her lips twitch, more amused than annoyed. "Plain speech, is it? Should have expected as much. Very well. We're sending Mr. Chavez to New York because they asked for him specifically. He has a mentor who works in-house who recommended him. Besides, they're looking to expand into non-fiction and they need someone to oversee the—"

"I could have done that." I blink and the warmth burns my exhausted eyes. I know my tone is disrespectful. The complaint is petty.

She nods at my interruption. "You could have, but I would hate to see you wallow in non-fiction when you've guided so many best-selling novels. The immersive worlds you help create speak for themselves."

Pulling at the hem of her jacket, she waits as if expecting another interruption.

I don't speak. I sit here with a foggy brain and sore body, wishing I'd had the courage to wake Nickie up and properly say goodbye before I snuck out of her hospital room like some kind of disreputable walk of shame.

"We'll be replacing both you and Mr. Chavez here because you'll be moving into a new role."

She pauses again. Maybe it's self-control, knowing I'm

too annoyed to be polite, but I keep my mouth shut and lift a hand, willing her to get on with it already.

"I'm disappointed with the slop we've been handed from agents this year, hopefully you'll have something better to work with after the first of the year. I've considered sending you and Emily to conferences to meet with authors directly. Something tells me you could read authors better than they read themselves. You could point, and we'd start designing the cover for our next bestseller. I haven't decided yet if that would work. You might inadvertently send them all away crying."

"It's not my job to hand out cookies."

"And we're not a bakery." She leans over the table, still ignoring her seat. "You rip manuscripts to shreds and stitch them back together without a scar. You're phenomenal."

I know I should say thank you, but it feels like a setup. She hasn't concluded the "moving into a new role" teaser. There's a hammer left to fall.

Mrs. Emmerson finally sits in the high-back leather chair. She adjusts her folder and arranges a pen above it with precise margins on either side. With her gaze on the wall clock, she takes a slow breath, chest rising. She looks at me with a smile. "I'm leaving. I met with corporate last night and turned in my resignation. I recommended they replace me in-house and told them to hire you. They're prepared to approve the offer as soon as I send word of your acceptance."

CEO of Lakeview Publishing.

There's a curve ball I wasn't expecting.

He swings. He strikes.

My fingers tighten on the pen. *Click. Click.* My boss of six years watches me, a tug of a secret smile brightening her face. What does she see?

She'll be disappointed if she expected gratitude.

I offer nothing.

"I have the details printed here. I know how you prefer to hold the final documents." She gives a full, satisfied smile and turns her attention to her folder, as if the whole thing is settled. Maybe it is—for her.

For me, though?

An official title, a corner office with windows, corporate's instant approval... it all lands with a soft thud. A stick tossed in tall grass. *Whoosh.* I watch it sail past with no urge to chase it.

Should I want this? Somewhere between Lauren's hug and praying beside Nickie's hospital bed, my foundation shifted.

I'm an editor. I don't think I want to run a company.

I improve stories. She says I tear them apart, but I don't. I dig into what's there and pull it out. I find the truth and expose it. I don't create anything. I find what's hidden and polish until it's so beautiful you can't walk by without noticing.

Despite the sluggish thoughts of my exhausted and drugged brain, I have enough clarity of what I want from life to ask, "Why?"

Before she answers, I think I know—she finally knows what she wants.

I answer my own question before she does. "You burned out, didn't you?"

"Of course not, with Dean retiring next year, we've decided it's time for—"

"Because you didn't have the time as CEO."

"But don't you see?" Her excitement is palpable. "That's why you're perfect. You don't have a family to distract you from the company. Imagine where you'll take it."

Her words rush over me like a waterfall and it's not gentle. Something hard and painful pinches in my chest. I will not give the best years of my life to a company in place of a warm family. If there was ever a doubt of what I wanted, it's crystal clear now.

"I'll think about it." I slowly stand, clenching my jaw against the swelling in my knee. "I'm going home early to give it some thought." Leaning across the table, I take the file she offers. "I'll give you my answer on Monday."

My phone buzzes. I ignore it like I have all after-noon. I pass Emily and Randy in the hallway and offer polite excuses as I keep walking. As I slowly make my way down twelve flights of stairs because elevators are boxes of death, I finally pull out my phone. Two missed calls from Mom, one from Dad, and a slew of texts.

Diana: Hey cousin, I guess you felt well enough to fly? I'm worried about you. Please call us when you have a minute. We love you.

Cordy: LANDS TO THE LIVING, MARK!

Cordy: I cannot believe you left her at the hospital. You. Left. Nickie!

Cordy: You do not have permission to call me as an emergency contact FROM AN AMBULANCE, freak everyone out, and then slip away during the night.

Cordy: I hope you heal quickly so that I can push you down a snowy hill and watch you roll into one of those man-sized snowballs.

Cordy: You're probably at work in a wrinkle-free button-up pretending you're too busy to read these and that just makes me madder. Livid. Boiling.

Cordy: You're a terrible person, and I hope you know how much we love you because if you weren't already in another state I would punch you.

Cordy: Maybe I will. I'm looking up flights right now.

Nathan: The sisters are upset, man. I'm sure you're fine or you wouldn't have left. Not sure if they're more worried about your health or because you didn't elope with Nickie. Tough crowd to please over here. Send proof of life ASAP.

I reply with a hand waving emoji to Nathan.

Cordy: Gilbert says to leave you alone for a few days, but whatever. Please call someone to let us know you're not dead. Even though we hate you. Because we really, really love you even though you're the worst.

Thumb hovering, I stare at the screen while waiting on the curb for my ride.

In the back of the car, I swipe through my contacts and text a friend from church.

Mark: Hey, Dan, are you hosting the New Year's gathering again this year? So, this might sound a little out of the blue, but I'm seriously looking for a date. If you happen to know a godly, grounded woman who's open to something real, would you keep me in mind?

18

———

# INTERLUDE

## Wednesday, December 27

*Bing!*

Dan: Yes! You've given Marlene the gift of the decade. She's got at least four women in mind starting with Abigail. You free for dinner Friday?

> Mark: I'd love to meet her. Early dinner works best for me. You have a place in mind?

Dan: Let me chat with the wife and get back to you. I'll text the address. Plan to meet her there when you get off work.

> Mark: Are you arranging a blind date, just like that?

Dan: You'll be fine. Abigail's great.

*Bing!*

Mark: Hey, Corbin, I'm not going to be able to meet for racquetball this week. I was in an accident and healing from whiplash. Sorry, man.

Corbin: Nooo! We're doomed without you.

Mark: Nah, you've still got Evan. I'll come cheer you to victory.

Corbin: Sure. Glad you're okay, bro. This was in Nebraska? At your sister's?

Mark: Cousin's. Yeah. I'm back now, just won't be up to speed for a while.

Corbin:  See you at Bible study?

Mark: Yeah. Hey, this might sound a little out of the blue, but I'm seriously looking for a date. If you happen to know a godly, grounded woman who's open to something real, would you keep me in mind?

Corbin: Bro, really? Yes! About time. I know the perfect girl for you. You want her number?

Mark: She won't think it's weird if I call her?

Corbin: Yeah, you're right. I'll have Rachel invite her to the Y sometime soon. You could meet her then. Her name's Trisha.

Mark: Appreciate it.

Corbin: I knew it. I always told Rachel you'd wake up one of these days, and when you did, LOOK OUT!

Corbin: *GIF of Keanu Reeves blowing kisses to a room full of people.*

Mark: Don't do that. I'm asking for your input because I trust your judgment.

Corbin: You're right. I'll be cool...

Mark: That you have to say it does not convince me you're being cool. I admire the relationship you and Rachel have. It makes sense. I'd like to have someone like that in my life.

Corbin: Rachel's one in a million. But I know what you mean. We'll introduce you to Trisha. No pressure.

## Thursday, December 28

*Bing!*

Unknown: I'm not sure if texting is allowed after you vanished to the airport, but I miss your face. Wondering if we're still friends. So. Hi.

Mark: Is this Nickie?

Nickie: I sluiced your number from your cousins.

Mark: *GIF of Inigo Montoya, "I do not think it means what you think it means."*

Nickie: Ack. Here I was trying to be funny and casual and ruined the punchline. SLEUTH. I promise I'm smart. Please don't judge me. I sleuthed your number. Because I'm an intelligent human adult who knows how to talk words and find facts about stuff.

Nickie: What are you thinking? Your response is too slow, and you're leaving me here feeling stupid.

Mark: I'm laughing, and even lying on the bed it makes everything hurt.

Nickie: You know what would help with that?

Mark: Not wearing seatbelts?

Nickie: That thing saved your life. How about staying off icy roads and telling airplanes they can wait?

Mark: I have a lovely bruise all the way across my chest.

Nickie: I imagine you have a lovely chest regardless of the bruise.

Mark: If I said that to you, would I be in trouble?

Nickie: You could try and see what happens.

Mark: Are you sitting down?

Nickie: I'm in Grandma's recliner with an icepack behind my neck and a hot pad on my back.

Mark: Okay. Here goes.

Nickie: I'm ready.

Mark: I'm not sure if you are.

Nickie: Definitely. I hate suspense.

Mark: I like boobs.

Mark: See… now you're not responding. Am I in trouble?

Nickie: I'm laughing, and it hurts. I'm also concerned that you're on something a little too strong?

Mark: I wish. Just very, very tired.

Mark: I'm sorry I wasn't brave enough to say goodbye.

Nickie: Me too.

Mark: I hurt all over, but leaving the way I did hurts the most. If I could do it over, I would have stayed. To make sure you were okay.

Nickie: Because you're worried about my health.

Mark: Sure.

Nickie: Well. I'm worried about your… health too.

Mark: Thank you for sluicing my number.

Nickie: You're not going to let that go, are you?

Mark: Not for many years, no. And then every decade I'll bring it up with perfect comedic timing, and we'll laugh about it together.

*Bing!*

John: I know I slept in. But please don't shovel the snow. It's the one thing that makes me feel like I'm pulling my weight around here.

Nickie: What? It was done when Grandma and I left. Grandpa is in so much trouble!

John: He says it wasn't him.

Nickie: Don't believe anything he says. He's squirrelly.

John: His alibi checks. You can cross examine when you get back.

Nickie: You're saying the snow mysteriously disappeared from our property and nobody knows anything about it? Do you need anything from downtown? G's perm's nearly dry and we're heading home.

John: Sour cream.

Nickie: I bought sour cream two days ago.

John: I ate it all. And corn chips. Or don't, but you should know I ate what was left. So don't sue me when you need it for something. FYI Gil and I are playing at a gig tonight and tomorrow. When do you go back to work?

Nickie: Next week.

John: What if you didn't? You look terrible.

Nickie: What if you stopped eating my snacks? I'll be fine.

*Bing!*

Dr. Kendrick: I feel like I'm the last to hear about your accident. Nobody told me until Darren asked me to cover for you tomorrow. I'm so sorry that happened. I'm more than happy to reschedule your appointments and work your shifts as long as you need. Or we'll have Darren call in a sub.

Nickie: Thanks, I'll be all right.

Dr. Kendrick: Are you sure? Can I bring you anything?

Nickie: My family's got it covered. See you at work next week.

*Bing!*

Nickie: Hey, Mark... You there?

Nickie: I know I shouldn't be texting this late. I hope you're sleeping peacefully. I miss you.

Mark: Hey, what's up?

Nickie: I'm sorry I woke you up.

Mark: It's all good. Talk to me.

Nickie: I keep seeing the moment before impact. Every time I close my eyes, my diamond bracelet flashes across my vision, and I can't breathe.

Mark: I wish I could hold you.

Nickie: I wish you could too.

Mark: Are you home?

Nickie: Yeah, standing in the kitchen.

Mark: If I were there, I'd make you a cup of tea. Can you do that? Sit and drink something?

Nickie: Yeah. How are you? Are you okay?

Mark: Not really. I had a dream or something when I blacked out. It was too real to be made up, but then they put us in two different ambulances, and my claustrophobia took over. I remember every detail, but it's also a foggy memory. How does that make sense?

Nickie: Depersonalization, it's a trauma response. Like how I can still see the fog on the edge of the windshield and the snowflakes silhouetted against the truck's lights. I hear how you called my name, but it's almost as if I'm watching a movie of someone else's memory. It replays over and over, stuck on repeat.

Mark: You could try writing it down. Let the paper hold the memory so you don't have to.

Nickie: Is that what you did? I don't want you stuck on repeat either.

Mark: I will now because I just thought of it. Sometimes it's easier to help other people than ourselves, isn't it? Thank you for texting me.

## Friday, December 29

*Bing!*

John: Did you order donuts delivered?

Nickie: Did you portal us to another town? Hadley Springs doesn't deliver donuts.

John: Donuts are here. I didn't buy them. But I'm eating them, want me to bring you one?

Nickie: Donuts in bed! Best day ever. Bring milk.

John: Do you want the flowers too? Dr. K brought over a pretty vase while you were sleeping.

Nickie: Oh, jeez. Fine. Bring them too.

*Bing!*

Mark: Nickie! This book I'm working through is hilarious. You're going to read it when it comes out.

Nickie: Well, good morning, sunshine. What's this book about?

Mark: Dragon slayers, wicked queens, a prince.

Nickie: Pass. Is it at least a kissing book? Tell me there's a happily ever after.

Mark: *GIF of Cary Elwes smiling.*

Nickie: Is that a yes?

Mark: It could be. So far FMC is in a dungeon.

Nickie: FMC?

Mark: Female main character.

Nickie: FMC in a dungeon doesn't sound hilarious.

Mark: It's comedy gold! At least it will be when I'm done with it.

Nickie: You're a book magician.

Mark: I am.

Nickie: Can you make sure your FMC does something for herself? If she's being dragged off by a troll, can she at least throw a rock up his nose? And please no fainting.

Mark: They have to faint. Corsets are too tight.

Nickie: Please no.

Mark: Corsets are tight, they don't have good shoes, and their dispositions are too weak. The prince is on his way to save her. She'll be fine.

Nickie: Now you're messing with me. This book sounds terrible.

Mark: I told you it was hilarious, not that it wasn't terrible.

Mark: Hypothetical question. If I was the boss of a publishing imprint, what would you say?

Nickie: Hypothetically?

Mark: Not so much.

Nickie: Then I say, of course Mark Brader is the boss. It's the next step in his world domination plan. Run a company, procreate, take over the world.

Mark: Wow, sure. I have too much to tell you, can I call?

Nickie: I thought you'd never ask.

## Sunday, December 31

*Bing!*

Mark: Hey beautiful. How was your day?

Nickie: The best.

Mark: Saving lives again?

Nickie: Not today! Rollover accidents grant me a few days off. Lucky me.

Mark: Feeling okay?

Nickie: No. Whiplash is a beast. Tell me something exciting.

Mark: Yesterday was my birthday.

Nickie: Come on! You mean we talked about everything and everyone except about how it was your birthday? Are you older and wiser now?

Mark: You will always have me beat there. One year to thirty.

Nickie: Thirty and flirty.

Nickie: Sorry, I've been living with grandparents too long. That was a weird thing to say. It rhymes so it came out. Please tell me I'm not the only dorky person in this conversation.

Mark: No can do. I walked a mile on a treadmill, so I'm pretty much a rockstar.

Nickie: That's adorable. I walked from John's car to a church pew and back again, but treadmills are cool.

Mark: You're a woman among women.

Nickie: Did you make a decision about the job?

Mark: Mostly. I'm wondering what kind of freedom I'd have. We don't need to be known as the publishing house that overworks their employees. If I insisted we get a full week off for Thanksgiving, Christmas, Easter, and three extra weeks throughout the year would they sack me?

Nickie: Not if your output matches or exceeds what came before. Your employees would love you. I think you should walk in on your first day with a Darth cape and theme music and tell everyone to go home because you're restructuring the whole operation into a 100% remote company.

Mark: Sorry, you lost me at "Darth cape." I assume you meant Vader? Darth is a title for Sith lords, not a name. Darth Vader, Darth Maul, Darth Sidious, Darth Tyranus…

Nickie: Is it short for Tyrannosaurus Rex? Wouldn't Darth Rex be easier for everyone?

Mark: Darth Rex would be an excellent Sith name. Intimidating, powerful. Especially juxtaposed with Count Dooku. With a name like that, no wonder he went to the dark side.

Nickie: Your attempt to out-geek me was successful, and I feel zero shame at my ignorance. Whatcha doing?

Mark: Sitting in a hot tub.

Nickie: You're not.

Mark: Am too.

Mark: *Image of bubbling water.*

Nickie: Really? I don't even get a picture of your face?

Mark: I'm not wearing a shirt. I didn't know if we were that kind of friends yet.

Nickie: "Yet," he says. Bahahaha. So I'll get a shirtless picture someday?

Mark: Now you've made it weird.

Nickie: Hardly. I'm not the one dropping "yets" all over the place. Tell me about your date with Abigail. Is Dan now the best man for the wedding?

Mark: She didn't show.

Nickie: Egads! Did you cry?

Mark: I waited ten minutes then I ordered a car to take me home. Wanna watch a movie?

Nickie: Ten minutes isn't long. What if she was running late?

Mark: If she's ten minutes late and didn't call, we're not a match.

Nickie: Did you call her when she didn't show up?

Mark: No.

Nickie: What if she got the time confused then sat for an hour waiting on you?

Mark: Are you trying to make me feel bad? She didn't show up! Strike. Next.

Nickie: You're a hard one to please. I think you should call her.

Mark: I don't want to call her. I want to watch a movie with you. Do you have time? I'm skipping the New Year's parties in favor of sleep this year.

Nickie: Sounds heavenly. But I get to pick. Get out of the tub and call me when you're dressed.

19

---

# NICKIE

## TUESDAY, JANUARY 2

My desk at the clinic is cluttered. I quickly put away stray pens and wipe away the crumbs from lunch. Before I see my next patient, I shoot a text to Mark about the values of karaoke. We've been arguing the merits of different party games since yesterday afternoon. Not sure how we got on this topic, but his immediate response has me smiling again as I tuck the phone in the pocket of my maxi peasant skirt. Gotta love a skirt with pockets that go on for days.

Mark and I talked on the phone for three hours on New Year's Eve, chatting through *My Fair Lady*, both of us ignoring the clock as it ticked past midnight. While debating whether to send a good-morning text the next morning, my phone pinged with an apology from Mark for keeping me up so late.

Of course I forgave him.

Those last few days at home went quickly, and despite the one late evening, I've been sleeping ten to twelve hours a night and napping every afternoon as I recover. John drove me to work today—my first day back—and I've got to say, I don't hate the chauffeur idea. Though I'd still trade this concussion for my car. I'm doing alright physically, but I have to keep reeling in my wayward thoughts. Damaging thoughts reliving the accident and the thrilling thoughts involving this new relationship.

What's a word for that odd heart pressure when you're excited but cautious, knowing you might be too enthralled with the nuances of another person? An alluring magic of a shared happiness.

I've never been so obsessed with checking my phone. It's been ten days since our date, eight days since we sat on my porch in the middle of the night, and seven days since Mark posed an outrageous rhetorical question about me moving across the country for a husband.

A confusing question. No matter how I lay it out, I don't believe he was legitimately asking. I think what he meant was, "Do you and I have a chance?" Then he didn't want to hear the answer, so he bolted.

I say we do.

Mark and I have a chance.

Despite the newness of this development, I sense untapped potential. Even as he's in Arizona scheduling dates, AKA wife interviews. Good grief. Even as I care for my aging grandparents far away in Nebraska, and he's about to accept a huge promotion today. None of that scares me.

Ten days of his face in my brain, and I'm stupidly happy. He might pretend to set me in the friend zone, but I'm holding on to the symptoms that tell a different story. Like how Mark didn't call that girl, Abigail, when she was a few minutes late, and how he calls *me* during his lunch break as if there's no one he'd rather talk to.

If Mark didn't care so much, why did he run? He's got a thick skull for someone who claims to know so much about character desires, motives, and—How did he phrase it?—intrinsic motivation? He'll analyze a manuscript and pull the perfect strings for a satisfying ending, but he won't acknowledge what's happening right under his nose.

Experiencing a traumatic event together can form a bond between two people, so I warn my heart to tiptoe. My face can't take the hint though. I walk around smiling at the clouds. The world is brighter. The snow is more beautiful. The stars shimmer with gusto.

This morning, we removed the stitches from the side of my forehead, and the wound is covered by my hair in a gentle side braid. I refresh the schedule on the laptop and pause when I see Diana Weston listed as my next patient. They must have let her in as a walk-in. Symptoms include fatigue, headache, nausea, starving all the time, weight gain, and urine test reveals hormone levels at... Oh dear.

Diana raises her head from a novel when I step into the exam room. Wearing a loose floral shirt draped over black leggings, a brave smile brightens her face only a moment before she bursts into tears.

I open my arms, and she falls into me with a tight embrace.

She speaks between sobs. "How... did... this... happen?"

I struggle to restrain laughter. "Well, friend, when a man and a woman love each other—"

Diana's sniffles turn into a laugh as she pushes me away. She grabs a tissue from the box on the counter. "Now we know why I'm still fat."

"You're not—"

"Shut up, Nickie. I'm still fat. Haven't lost an ounce since Jack. Gained some too, but Nathan threw away our scale so I can't say for sure. I refused to look when I stood on your hallway scale. You really can't put that somewhere more discreet with three-inch numbers to shout at everyone spying through the lobby? Gosh, Nickie, I'm so scared. Can you order me an ultrasound?"

"Do you know the first day of your last period?"

"I haven't had one since before Jack. I'm still nursing, and he's barely seven months old." Diana blows her nose.

"You missed his six-month well-baby appointment. Are you skipping that on purpose?"

She waves a hand over her shoulder and mutters, "He's fine."

"Did you take a home pregnancy test?"

"I don't need to." She grabs my hand and presses it to her side under her ribcage. "Press harder, right— Feel that nudge? How can we feel that already? That's a foot! Lord, help me."

Her hands release mine to scrub her pale face. "We were so careful. I promise you we haven't messed around once without protection. Not even once, except..." Her eyes grow wide. "No," she whispers. "No! It can't be possible."

With her palms against her soft stomach she looks through me, and the rest of the color drains from her face. "Five weeks after Jack was born. Please tell me it's not possible. That would mean..." She shakes her head in disbelief.

Now's not really the time to explain God and science to my shocked friend. But yes, anything is possible.

I take the wall calendar and set it on the padded examination table. She stands beside me, and the clean paper crinkles as we lean over the calendar. Diana flips backward and points to June second. "Jack was born here." She counts forward five weeks. "The *you know what* must have been July seventh. Nathan is in so much trouble for this."

Laughing softly, I pull my braid over my shoulder. "Sure, if that helps you feel better."

"It doesn't." Her finger taps the weeks as she counts forward, furiously flipping the pages as she goes. "Thirty-eight, thirty-nine, forty. That puts her due date April thirteenth."

I gently take her hand and scoot it up. "All your babies come early."

She drags her finger down the page. "April thirteenth. She might bake longer than the rest."

I push it back to the beginning of the month. "She?"

"Please let me have another girl," Diana whispers.

I know she wasn't expecting another baby, especially not so soon, but a part of me softens at the idea of my dearest friend privileged to bring another life into the world. He's working another miracle. The precious life of a human child is being knit together in Diana's womb. *Lord, grant me this blessing someday.*

"Diana." I wait until she pulls her gaze from the calendar. The dark smudges both from exhaustion and rushed makeup don't detract from the vibrant youth in her blue eyes. "Remember the first time we met?"

She sniffs. "It was in this room, wasn't it?"

I nod, smiling. "You had Landon, who wouldn't stop fussing."

"You suggested I nurse him while you looked in his ear."

"Yeah, do you remember what you said that day?"

"I don't even remember where I left my coffee this morning."

I return the calendar to January and hang it on the wall. "You were my first patient as a fully licensed doctor, so I'll remember for the both of us. You told me that you'd been up all night, and even though he didn't have a fever, you knew something was wrong."

"Well, sure. Any mother can tell when something's wrong with her baby."

I shake my head trying not to let myself get emotional. "I've seen too many neglected kids to believe that anymore. There's a certain brand of mothers, like you, that pay attention. Do you remember what you said later when we found out God had blessed you with twins?"

"Um, probably, 'I can't do it. It's too much.'"

"Yet here you are. So you must have grown stronger. Then came Lisa."

"And she was more than I could handle."

"Except you got stronger again. Then Jack was born."

An overwhelming sense of love and compassion flows from Diana at the mention of her last surprise baby. "I don't know what we'd do without him." She wraps her arms around her waist and closes her eyes. "We keep meaning to schedule Nathan's appointment and be done having babies, but each kid makes our family more complete. I can't imagine not having a single one of them. It's not that I don't want this baby, but I don't want to go through this again. I'm so freaking tired." Her tears are so fast they drip from her chin before she catches them.

I pass her another tissue. "Mom says we're not supposed to say freaking."

"What is God thinking? He's got to know this is terrible timing."

"Maybe you should have thought of that before getting busy five weeks postpartum, which I officially do not recommend."

"Your advice is neither welcome nor helpful." She

stares me down, and I return her gaze until she slumps her shoulders.

I press my foot on the trashcan lever to open the lid for her snot-filled tissue.

"Nathan is going to faint."

"I think they prefer *black out* or something manlier. Who's with the kids right now?"

"I asked Nathan to take a longer lunch break so I could have a lunch date with you because it had been so long since we've had a chance to talk."

"Diana!"

"I know, I'll tell him. I need a minute."

My phone pings, and although I would never check my phone when I'm with a patient, I rationalize that it's just Diana, and before I know it, I'm smiling at my screen and typing out a quick reply to Mark.

"Who's that? Why're you grinning like that?"

"Hmm?" I glance up, and she's eyeing me as if I've taken the last ice-cream bar from the freezer—which I never do because John eats everything.

"You look—" And then the phone is in her hand. "Mark! You're texting Mark! I knew it!" She turns and flaps her elbows when I try to grab my phone. "Do you love him?"

"Diana, what the heck?"

"Got something to hide? Let me see! Mark doesn't tell me nothing, and he's been flirt-texting you this whole week! Are you flexting my cousin?"

We scrabble for the phone, and she's wedged herself in the corner between the examination table and the wall.

"Argh!" I take an elbow to the gut.

"Oof!" The curly cords of the otoscope and other diagnostic tools attached to the wall get tangled in her arm. "Careful, I'm pregnant!"

"And I have a concussion. Give it back, fiend."

As she twists away, the black cords pull tighter around her. "Ahh! I'm stuck." Somehow she's caught herself in a tangle of cords in the tight space. "Do you like him? Really, really like him?"

"Yes." I snatch the blood pressure cuff and wrap it around her torso and both arms until she's immobile. Not hiding my smile, I pluck the phone from her, releasing a loud, "Hah!" at my entangled friend.

A knock sobers me quickly as Preston opens the door. Confusion creases his features when he finds me standing in the middle of the room. His gaze catches on the side of my head, and I self-consciously pat my hair and feel a section that's been pulled from my braid.

"What's going on in here?" he hisses.

A squeak from Diana exposes her position, and he opens the door to find her caught against the wall like a spider's next meal. "Good afternoon, Dr. Kendrick," Diana says with a straight face. "I'm going to be a mom again. Who knew, right? Number seven, here we come!"

And despite the raw emotion and the real work we both know is lurking behind the corner, when Diana looks at me with flushed cheeks and hair askew, there's a kindred bond of friendship and a *knowing* that zings between us.

Preston steps into the room, the embodiment of professionalism. Diana, trying too hard to keep from laughing, accidentally releases an unladylike snort. It's the catalyst that sets both of us into full, shoulder-shaking, leg-weakening laughter. I sink into a chair and let Preston untangle her.

"I guess I should call Nathan," Diana says, eying me

over Preston's hunched shoulder. "Will you call him now? Let's just rip off that Band-Aid."

I send out the call and put it on speakerphone.

"Hello," Nathan answers, sounding winded. "Nick, is my wife still with you?"

"You're on speaker, Nate. Diana has something fun to tell you."

"Can it wait? We have a situation here. Ow, Jack, stop it."

Preston turns Diana in a slow circle, carefully unraveling one of the cords.

"Nathan, honey, guess who's gonna have another baby?" Diana asks.

"Um, I don't know. Melissa? It's really not— Jack, hold still."

"It's us!" Diana speaks loudly from across the room. "I'm pregnant again." She lifts her arm as Preston guides her around the blood-pressure cord. "And you're the father!"

"Good one, babe. Can you please come home? I've got a meeting at one fifteen."

Preston shakes his head, but doesn't join the conversation as he reattaches the equipment neatly on the wall.

"We can get you in for an ultrasound this afternoon," I say. "When can you be here?"

"Wait." Jack gurgles, and there's a jingle of a rattle. "You're not kidding. Diana's— But we haven't— Is it Jesus?"

"Oh, good grief." Diana marches across the room and takes the phone from me. "I'll be home in a minute. Find that tub of cheese puffs. That'll distract the kids so you can process. See you soon. Love you. Bye." She hangs up. "Well, it's been lovely. We should do this again sometime. I'll call the office as soon as Nathan and I can both come back."

She jams her finger into my shoulder. "Don't think I've

forgotten about that other thing. Just because I have seven children doesn't mean I'm not interested in you and Mark. This is my one shot to get you into the family."

She grabs her purse and waltzes out, leaving Preston standing with hands on hips, mouth in a straight line, staring like I'm an expired food he can't decide is spoiled or not.

"Sorry about the noise. That was unprofessional."

His cheeks tighten in a frown. "Mark from the gala?"

"Yeah."

Preston's green eyes reveal nothing. His chest rises, filling out his fitted blue button-up. "Doesn't he live in Arizona?"

"Inconvenient, isn't it?"

"You're going to try a long distance relationship?"

"I'm not thinking about that. I'm going to enjoy Hadley Springs, and see what happens. It's not up to me where Mark lives."

"Sandy is waiting for you in room two." His gaze roves over my head and down to my shoes. "Check yourself in the mirror before you go in. You look like you've lost a wrestling match."

20

# NICKIE

## THURSDAY, JANUARY 11

HAMILTON SOUNDTRACK—HELPLESS

I drag myself in the house after another full day at the clinic. Gilbert's truck is parked in the street, so Hadley Strings must be practicing in the attic studio. I shut the front door carefully in case they're recording.

A piano and cello duet floats through the vent above my head. While I toe off my leather boots, I swipe to answer the incoming video call from Mark. Something buzzes through me when I see his face. He's in the backseat of a car, riding through sunny Phoenix. His face is vibrant and flushed. I already have his schedule memorized and know he's returning from his racquetball scrimmage.

"Hey, beautiful," he says with a smile, and I'm sunk.

I haven't nursed a crush like this since middle school. Logically, I know what is happening to my hormone-controlled brain. Mark is handsome, pleasant, funny. His confidence is magnetic. When I see and hear him, my brain releases neurotransmitters like dopamine that insist I need more. Cortisol increases with the excitement and gives me a boost of energy. In turn, my serotonin decreases which contributes to my obsessive infatuation with this man.

It's all hormonal. Hormones that control my feelings. Feelings that can lie. But even when I know about norepinephrine and its role in increasing my focus, I can't ignore how wonderful it feels. Who wouldn't want to stay in the euphoric state caused by the smile of another person?

Is it addictive? Maybe. Is it harmful? The prognosis is still unclear. What I do know is that I've caught something serious, and I'm not looking for a cure.

"You okay?" Mark speaks again, and I blink out of my *why am I so happy?* diagnosis.

"Yeah, just great to see you." I shrug off my coat and pull the yellow sticky note off the wall. I read it on the way to the kitchen.

*Nick! Stop it with the snow. I missed one weekend! I promise I'm not a failure. -John*

I chuckle and show the note to Mark. "John's marbles are a little loose. He keeps fussing at me about the snow. It's odd though. There's snow in the morning when I leave, no snow when I get back. But he says he's not moving it. We have a nice neighbor I guess. What do you make of that?"

"Why does John care as long as it's being done?"

I shrug and press the switch on my electric kettle. "Doesn't matter to me. I mean, sure, I'd like to thank them. Although I enjoy walking on a clear sidewalk, I'd explain that John or I can do it. John's a bit inconsistent with all his trips with the band." The crumbled paper makes a tiny ball that I chuck into the recycling bin.

"Hang on a sec." Mark thanks his driver and makes his way through the hotel lobby.

"Want to give me a tour of your fancy pad?"

"Um, sure. Prepare to be underwhelmed." He waves at

someone by the front desk and enters a long hallway. "This is the gym. Very fancy." He turns the camera, and I take in a bare bones workout room with two treadmills and a rack of weights.

"So fancy. Worth the membership?"

"Yep, it smells as good as it looks too. There's the pool and hot tub across the hallway."

I barely catch a glimpse of the small pool before he drops the phone to his side. "*Hola*, Rosita."

"*Bienvenido a casa, mijo. Te preparé unas conchitas. ¿Me trajiste un libro nuevo?*"

Mark laughs. "*Gracias! Me encantan conchitas.* Ehh... *no libro... necesito tiempo.*"

He speaks Spanish? I learn something new about this guy every day. His words are hesitant, but I'm still impressed. I have no idea what they're talking about. Something about a book, I think. *Tiempo* is time. Thank you... Book something something... time. That's all I catch.

The woman sighs. "Okay, okay. You need anything?"

Mark approaches a cleaning cart. From what I can tell, he's gathering a supply of rags and tiny toiletries. "Hey, mister," I interrupt as I sink into the couch next to dozing Grandpa Jeffrey. "You can call back later if you like."

Rosita gasps and her face comes into view. "*¡Ay, mírala!* Who is this?"

I think she's holding the phone now. I see a large forehead and jet-black hair pulled into a high knot. "*¿Quién es esta muchacha? Sé que no es tu hermana por cómo te sonrojas.*" With laughter she passes me to Mark.

"This is Nickie, um, *mi amiga*, Nickie."

The woman continues to laugh. "Little screen girl. *No bueno. Búscate una de carne y hueso que te dé tortillas y amor.*" Rosita pushes close to Mark and waves. "*Hola,* Nickie. You bring food, *sí?* He skinny, skinny."

Mark's eyes widen before moving away from her. "Alright, Rosita. Get on with you. *Ándale.*"

"*Toma.*" She pushes a plastic food container against his chest. "*Conchitos para ti.*"

"*Buenas noches,* Rosita." Then he's in his room, leaning against the door. "Sorry. I forgot to warn you about the greeting party."

"I think she likes you."

"I've been introduced to all of her granddaughters. I *think* all of them. I can't keep track. But it's hard to say no to the food she brings. It's really good."

"Is that legal? Cleaning ladies bringing food for single men?"

He shrugs and flops on the bed, arm behind his head. "I've been at this hotel for almost two years. It's not like she surprised me with a casserole on day one."

"You look tired."

A lazy smile fills his face. "Yeah, full day of work and racquetball with the guys. Not as tired as Grandpa there. Hey! Jeffrey!"

Grandpa snorts and sits up. "I'm ready."

Mark and I laugh, but Grandpa has already closed his eyes again.

"You know, Nickie. I was thinking about your situation."

"What situation is that?" I glance up as I hear Grandma making her way down the hallway.

"Your parents run a daycare. What if your grandparents spent part of each day there? Couldn't they be useful with the kids and in turn your mom could keep an eye on things? Joyce could read books or sit and watch the toddlers. Jeffrey could sing. Anyone can play peek-a-boo, you know? If your mom had space for them to sit somewhere and maybe a bed where they could take their naps, wouldn't it be useful for everyone?"

The rattle of Grandma's walker pauses. She's stopped at the entry from the hallway with furrowed brows and deep frown lines. "I'm not strong enough to hold the babies."

Sweet Joyce. "Mark's got a good point though, Grandma. You wouldn't have to hold the children to be useful. It sounds like a wonderful idea. If you're up for giving it a try, I'll talk to mom about it tonight."

"I could fold towels." Grandma continues her slow trek into the room. "Is that Mark on your phone?"

"Hi, Grandma Joyce," Mark raises his voice, and I angle the screen toward Grandma. We've been chatting almost daily. He and the grandparents are used to each other by now.

"Mark, honey, I was wondering if you've ever met the author Mandi Blake. You know many authors with your job, don't you?"

"I do, but I've never worked with Mandi."

"Oh. Well, if you meet her, I'd like to know if that poor girl is okay. I finished another one of her books, and it seems these cowboys keep getting into gun fights. Dawson and Asa and all those Blackwater men are in danger all the time. So I just wanted to ask if Mandi was in some kind of trouble?"

My book-saving, kid-wrangling, spreadsheet-building friend Mark wins more points for keeping a straight face. "Joyce, if I ever meet her, I'll find out for you. But I imagine she's fine. Readers like a little suspense. It sounds like you do too."

"Oh, no, dear. I only love a good kissing book."

"I'll remember that." Mark's natural grin pulls me in as

he holds my gaze. I'm helpless to stop these lovely feelings. Even as I internally scream, *It's nothing but silly hormones because he's got a nice face!*

The thunder of John speeding down the stairs precedes his entrance. "Hey, don't get comfortable. You 'bout ready to go?"

Grandpa lifts his head again. "I'm ready."

Taking Grandpa's soft hand in mine I lean onto his shoulder. "We're going to Aunt Jewels' for Thursday dinner. You're going to bed. We're going to party all night, and you'll turn into a pumpkin."

Cordelia Thompson and Gilbert appear behind John.

"I love pumpkins," Mark says.

"Is that Mark?" Cordy rushes across the room and plops onto the couch beside me. "Mark! I miss your face. Why don't you ever call *me* on video?"

"Because you're an ugly goose. You didn't answer my texts this morning either. Are you turning in the pitch for the Easter cookbook this week?"

"I'm not going to."

Mark sits up. "Cordy, *Christmas Comforts* is going to be a huge hit. This is the time to lean into the next project. Keep the momentum going."

"Yeah, but I don't want to. I'm tired."

I see so many thoughts rolling through Mark's expression, but I haven't known him long enough to really know what he's thinking. He breathes in slowly like when he dealt with Lauren's math escapade.

"You're tired," he repeats.

"Yeah, so we'll talk later. We're going to the Thursday thing. I'll tell Diana you said hi. K, bye." Cordy bounces off the couch, and in one burst has grabbed Gilbert's hand and pulled him out of the living room. "See you there!"

I'm not entirely sure what Cordy's talking about, but I know Mark's been coaching her career through the years. If he were here in bodily form, I imagine Cordy wouldn't have been able to breeze past their conversation.

Mark's face on a screen isn't enough. I want more. I want him here in this mix of family and friends. I slouch down into the cushions and cradle the phone in my lap. Mark says nothing as I study him.

John helps Grandma settle into her chair with a warm drink and reading lamp.

Mark smiles, but his fire has dimmed. "Goodnight, Nickie. Have fun." The energy he had a few minutes ago has snuffed out.

"Wanna watch a movie together tomorrow? I'll be off by four."

"Probably not this weekend. I've got a date with Trisha, men's Bible study Saturday morning, another date Saturday night. Abigail again."

I push a smile on my face. "Okay, well, have fun." I'm completely carefree and couldn't care less if my friend in Arizona wants to meet other women. He's going to spend the whole evening comparing them against an impossible list of Perfect Wife credentials anyway so *good luck with that, weirdo.*

"Thanks, talk to you later." His smile mimics mine as he ends the call.

Grandpa opens his eyes as I'm deciding whether or not to throw the phone through my front window. "That boy's in love with you."

"*Psh,* as he goes on two more dates this weekend?"

"As sure as chickens."

"Chickens what? As sure as chickens…"

"Eggs or thereabouts. I don't remember. Mark will come around. Sure as snow."

"Now you're making stuff up. Snow isn't sure and neither are chickens."

John tosses my coat on my lap. "Come on, sis. Let's go."

I pull my arms through my coat and follow John to the car. I don't like the spike of jealousy I have toward Trisha and Abigail, women that I've never met and have no right to hate. Is friendship with Mark worth pretending I don't care if he's seeing other people?

Let him see other people! Let him find a wife and leave me be. Hadley Springs is my home. I have my brother, my parents, grandparents, and a lifetime of community.

Riding silently next to John, I think about giving all of this up. If Mark earnestly pursued me, loved me, would I be willing to leave this?

The holiday lights in my quiet town blink at me through the streets. Yes. I would trade all of this for the right man. The admission shocks me.

Love is weird.

Though at the moment it's irrelevant. Mark can go on his dates, I'll keep enjoying Hadley Springs, and maybe he'll figure out what he actually wants. Because until he confirms his plan, it's not safe for me to dream. I'm falling for Mark, that much is clear, but I'm not yet willing to stick my neck out for a *sure as chickens*.

## 21

---

## MARK

### THURSDAY, JANUARY 18

Trisha Stone is waiting on the bench outside the racquetball courts. I recognize her long, dark hair flowing down her back in waves. I abruptly turn, and Corbin slams into my chest.

I shove him back and around the corner.

"Hey, man. What's that for?"

"Walk." I push him toward the locker rooms. "Why is Trisha here?"

He stops resisting and spins toward me with glee written all over his face. "She's here?"

"Shh." I lower my voice as I keep pushing us into the semi-privacy of the men's room. "I wasn't going to call her again. Why is she here?"

"Rachel said Trisha had a great time. Don't look at me like that. Rachel must've told her you'd be here. Just be your normal self. She'll love you."

I glance over my shoulder as if she'll materialize at any moment. "That's not part of the deal."

"What deal? You said you wanted to meet people."

"Yeah, I met her. Not to be disrespectful but, *I seen* what I needed to see."

"After one date? What did you even do? Dinner and a movie? How could you write her off so fast? Give it another shot."

"No, we hiked three miles around the Rio Salado area. She doesn't match the... never mind. I have an email drafted to let her down easy. Now she's going to watch us play racquetball like a spectator sport? Call your wife right now and make her come get her."

"Whoa," Corbin laughs, obviously not listening to me. "Mark Brader is scared? I didn't know it was possible."

"I care enough not to waste her time."

"So let's play ball. The others will be here soon. She's new to our group and is still making friends. She can hang out with the other wives."

"Perfect, so afterward we'll go to dinner with you and Rachel, Evan and his wife, all the other couples, then Trisha and me." I grip my safety glasses tightly by the strap, bouncing them against my leg, and dip my head to the floor. I breathe in on a count of four and hold it.

I'm in control of myself and only myself. Corbin is a good friend. His wife Rachel didn't mean any harm. Trisha isn't my enemy. I am safe. I'm not in control of anyone's feelings. I don't own the group. Anyone is welcome. I'm free to walk away anytime. I only have to do what I want to do, and since I want good friendships, I want to release this frustration.

I want to hit something. The tightness coiling inside me is about to burst.

"Thanks for the introduction. I appreciate it, Corbin, but I don't need an extended matchmaker. In the future, please, leave off after the intro. Now that she's here, don't be annoying about this, or I promise I will accidentally smash your face."

"Understood." Corbin cuts around me to the door, smirk still lingering.

A few other couples are waiting on the benches when we get back. Rachel is standing in front of Trisha and waves when she sees us. I've been playing here with the same group of guys from church for a year. Almost every Thursday we play, sometimes their wives come, and we'll often go for dinner afterward.

Trisha steps in for a side hug as I'm offering a handshake, and it's an awkward few seconds untangling. Her smile is kind. She's accommodating and agreeable. Too agreeable. Our date was flat because she never disagreed with me once. She carries herself well, she's friendly, interesting enough, but overall lacks ambition.

"So, what's the objective?" Trisha asks as I kneel to tighten the laces on my gym shoes.

Straightening, I settle the goggles against my face. There. Maybe if I tuck my shirt in and pull my shorts as high as they'll go, she'll realize I'm an unattractive dork and lose interest. For the first time in my life, I'm wishing I had a mouth guard to add to this ensemble.

"What's the objective? How do you win?" She's asking about racquetball, but I'd love to offer a different answer.

I lift the racquet in one hand, blue rubber ball in the other. "Hit the ball against the wall. Try not to get hit in the face."

"That's it?"

"Pretty much."

Evan claps as he arrives with his wife behind him, who

holds their infant son. "Who's ready to die?" He lifts his arms over his head like a hero of old.

We laugh at our friend. He's either the biggest geek on the planet, or the bravest man I know. Maybe both. He's past forty, usually comes in last place, plays the guitar, has a collection of kids, and runs a landscaping company.

Today he's wearing a blue striped sweat band across his head to keep his shaggy black hair out of his face. Matching sweat cuffs at his wrists. Name-brand jersey and shorts. Tube socks. Shiny new shoes.

He points to his toned bicep. "Check this out." It's an ink drawing of himself holding a racquet in one hand and a trophy in the other. "My son, Brandon, decorated my arm for the evening. You're all going down."

The women swarm his wife and take turns gushing over the baby. I pull the evening's tournament schedule from my pocket, and names are quickly written in for the starting match.

"How's the knee?" Corbin points to the elastic sleeve I'm wearing.

"It's better. I just don't want to re-injure it."

Trisha's beside me and places a hand on my shoulder. "What happened?"

"This dude got caught in a blizzard over Christmas."

I raise my eyebrows at Corbin's exaggeration. I'm fairly confident I didn't tell him the details about that night.

"Where did you find a blizzard?" Trisha tightens her grip on my shoulder. I reach for my gym bag as an excuse to move away from her.

"I have family in Nebraska." I unzip my bag and rifle through it for no reason. I check my phone, smile at a text from Nickie, and set it back down on the bench. "It wasn't really a blizzard, I mean, there was one earlier, but this was a mix of icy roads and an idiot in front of us. My driver did everything right, but sometimes it's out of your hands. She was hurt more than I was. We're both very fortunate. Come on." I slap Corbin on the back. "Let's play."

Soon my mind is in the game, and I'm free of every burden. Unlimited potential. Unlimited abundance.

I win my first and second matches.

The pop of the ball as it hits the wall, floor, or ceiling is all encompassing. The game is run by pure instinct at this point. There's no room for a single thought outside of where to place the racquet.

If only the rest of my life would roll this way. How can I harness this focus for Lakeview Publishing? The transition has been pretty great over all, but I won't see improved output for a few months yet.

*Project: Find a Wife* is running on schedule. Trisha doesn't match the profile. Abigail doesn't either, but that's not a problem. I already have a date arranged next week with one of Emily's friends.

I lunge the wrong direction as Evan's wild serve ricochets off the floor by my feet. The rubber torpedo explodes against my nose. Immediate pain bursts through my face, and I take a knee. A gush of warmth flows down my chin before I rip off my goggles.

Evan strips out of his shirt and holds it under my nose. "You're a regular fountain, man! So sorry." He stands and wrenches open the glass door. "Someone run get ice. Mark's busted his nose."

The pain is intense, far beyond a simple bloody nose. I wonder if this will compound any head injuries from the car accident. My whole body was sore, but my head seemed fine. I carefully make my way off of the court with Evan's shirt soaking up my life source.

Hands guide me to a bench. "I'm calling 911," Trisha says.

"No!" My voice sounds harsh. I carefully clear my throat and try again. "Get Corbin over here."

"I'm right here, dude."

I lower the shirt to show him my face. "What do you think?"

He squints and turns his head. "I have no idea. If it stops bleeding in a minute, we'll find out. I'm not a doctor."

I speak through the shirt again with a riot of pain popping through my skull. "Will you hand me my phone?"

Trisha presses my thumb against the sensor to unlock the phone. I swipe down my recent calls and press the video icon for Nickie.

She answers almost immediately. "Well, hello—Ahh, that's a lot of blood." Nickie's still in her clinic office. She turns her chair and the framed diplomas behind her blur on the screen. "Please tell me you didn't pick a fight with a racquetball and lose."

I start to smile, but seeing her face brings on a surge of longing, and I'm embarrassed to speak through the emotions. Crying over the phone to Nickie in front of all my friends isn't part of any plan. But I would like to know if I should seek medical attention or just ice my face.

"Hi." I try to move the shirt so I can show her my face, but I'm going to make a mess.

"Hey, um, your friend there." Nickie points behind me. "What's your name? With the dark hair?"

"I'm Trisha." Her hands come under mine and take the phone.

"Will you tell me what's going on?" Nickie asks.

"Mark's nose is bleeding."

Nickie nods. "And?"

"And he doesn't want me to call 911."

"That makes sense. And?"

Trisha shrugs. "That's all I know. He said he'd call a doctor."

"That would be me. Okay, hey, Mark, lean forward a little. Don't swallow that blood, it'll make you feel sick. Put ice on it. Pinch the bridge of your nose for a good ten minutes."

I try to follow her instructions, and when I touch my nose a shock of pain echoes, and I involuntarily cry out.

"Ope, okay. So there's some extra pain there. Breathe through your mouth. Try to put firm pressure on it. Trisha, find out if he feels a crunching when he touches his nose or if looks crooked at all?"

"I'm going to be sick." Trisha sets the phone on the bench and disappears behind me.

Corbin lifts the phone. "Hey, I'm Corbin. You his doctor friend?"

"That's me! Hi, Corbin. I really can't give you very good medical advice from here. Was it the ball or something else?"

Evan leans over my shoulder into Nickie's view. "It was the ball."

"Okay, then it's probably not broken, but don't take my word for it. If his nose looks bent, or if the bleeding hasn't stopped in ten minutes, I recommend you take him in. There's no call for an ambulance."

"I can take him," Trisha offers from somewhere behind me.

"No, thanks." I stare Corbin in the eyes, willing him to advocate for me. I don't want to be a huge jerk, but I don't want Trisha playing nurse. Ever. I don't need female friends when I'm trying to find a wife in Phoenix. Especially ones who can't handle the sight of blood.

Corbin offers a minuscule nod of understanding. "Thanks, Trisha. Rachel and I will take him wherever he needs to go. We'll catch you later."

"Here." Rachel crouches in front of me and offers a bag of ice. "Want this?"

No, I don't *want this*. I don't want any of this! *Lord Jesus, my face hurts.* I want to teleport to Nickie's porch and be held until my world's back under control. I take the ice from Rachel and see my fingers shaking.

"Mark," Nickie's voice softens. "Thanks for calling. I'll be praying for you. Send me an update tonight." Her face freezes on the screen a moment after she's ended the call.

I close my eyes and hold the ice to my face with Evan's soggy mess of a shirt around it. This was decidedly *not* part of the plan. If I could cry like a child and beg Nickie to come down here and still be a man, I would.

For now, I let my friends help me to a car, doing my best to act like I'm going to be okay and not like an editor whose characters have taken a red pen to their own story.

# 22

# NICKIE

## SUNDAY, JANUARY 21



I'm blocked in the middle of the pew with Mom and Dad on one side, Grandma and Grandpa on the other. They're each talking to someone else on their ends.

Briefly, I consider climbing over the pew in front as a means of escape. I'm tall enough that I could slink right over the top before anyone noticed. That'd be tricky in the skirt I chose today though. It's a vintage brown corduroy with matching vest.

That settles it. Pants for church henceforth, so I can sneak over or under these constricting pews.

A child's hand on my shoe startles me from my wayward thoughts. Lisa Weston looks up with her blond curls dangling free from the headband looped around her neck. Then she giggles and crawls past me under the pew. Lucky girl.

Hmm. I sit, resigned to wait while the adults finish their conversations. Of course, I'm an adult too. Otherwise I'd be following Lisa.

The noise is overwhelming with everyone talking at once and children running all over. I need a nap after being on call for the hospital the whole weekend.

I stand again and place my hand on Mom's shoulder. "Excuse me, please."

John's in the back with Gilbert and Cordy and a few others. When he catches my eye I mouth, *I'm walking home*, and sign the action with walking fingers in the air.

Outside, brilliant sunshine blinds me, reflecting off piles of dirty snow and damp salt-covered sidewalks. The Weston crew is gathered just past the door.

"One, two, three, four, five. Where's Lisa?" Diana tugs the blanket tighter around Jack, who's strapped to her chest in a baby carrier. "Nathan, have you seen Lisa? I thought she was right here."

"You can start walking, I'll find her." Nathan heads back inside. "Hey, Nick."

"She was under our pew just before I came out. Headed toward the front."

"Thanks."

I loop my arm into Diana's, and we follow the kids toward their street. They live about four blocks from the church, and I'm a few more past them. The winter air is fresh and invigorating today. It's a beautiful day to be outside.

My cell buzzes.

> Dr. Kendrick: I saw you're off the next couple days. Want to grab a movie?

"Seriously!" I groan and show Diana the text. "Why won't he take no for an answer?"

"You gotta give him credit for trying."

Nickie: Sorry, I'm pretty busy.

That taken care of, I tug on Diana's arm. "I have another problem."

"Mineral, animal, or vegetable?"

"Animal, definitely."

"Human or creature?"

"Creature." I laugh.

The kids crowd on what Diana has designated the *stopping square* where the two sidewalks intersect at the corner. She looks both ways. "Go ahead." The kids sprint across. "So, Mark?"

"Mark." I step over the running water near the curb.

"Shall I keep guessing or will you tell me, please?"

"I haven't heard from him in days, Diana. Has he talked to you recently?"

"What's recently? We don't talk all that often." She pushes her elbow into my side. "I'm not his girlfriend."

"Well, if you were trying to hurt my feelings, consider them hurt. He's got a spreadsheet you know, and I'm not on it."

"Aw, I'm sorry, friend. He'll come around. I really think he's in denial."

"Why though?" I push all my frustration into my voice and hide nothing from Diana. "I don't want to keep playing this game with him."

"What game?"

"What game?" I tug on the wrists of my perfectly tight gloves. "What game! The one where he acts like a boyfriend then dates other women, and I pretend it doesn't bother me. We text all the time. We video chat almost daily. He answers my calls with 'Hey, beautiful,' like he doesn't even know he's doing it—but you know he means what he says.

He doesn't do anything he doesn't want to do. Diana, I'm stupidly infatuated with your annoying cousin. Then! Silence. Nothing since Thursday."

"Oh, Nickie, you're worried about two days? That's nothing."

"It's something for how constantly we talk. And it's something because he might have broken his nose Thursday night."

"That I didn't know." Diana steps around an icy puddle on the sidewalk. "Nobody tells me anything!"

"I doubt he told anyone. I only got the call because he was spurting blood and needed to talk Trisha out of calling an ambulance."

"Who's Trisha?"

"We're not talking about Trisha."

"I am. Who's Trisha?"

"A *candidate*. But she's not a fit. He told me earlier last week."

"He tells you about his dates?"

"That's what I'm saying!" I nudge Landon and the boys to go ahead across the next street, and lower my voice. "How is Mark the best and the worst?"

"I know exactly what you mean. Everything he does is so... so... intentional. He's quick to help everyone then never lets us know when he needs help. His standards are so high nobody can keep up with him. But isn't that why we love him?"

"Exactly!" I grab Leo under the arms and boost him forward before I run into him. I want to march faster. "Mark's level of confidence makes me want to follow him around and see what amazing thing he'll do next. What am I going to do? What can I do that I'm not already doing? I like him so much, but I shouldn't need to convince him to be with me. If we're meant to be, I shouldn't have to force him... but... I wish..."

"Poop, or quit hogging the bathroom?"

"Diana!"

Leo runs away and shoves the back of his older brother, Landon. "Mom said poop!"

"Oh, good grief," Diana mutters. "Boys! Run home now and clean the table for lunch."

The boys zip off down the sidewalk.

Diana slows her steps, and I almost walk into her when she turns to look over her shoulder. "You too, Lauren. Get changed into play clothes and set out sandwich stuff for lunch."

I'd forgotten Lauren was there because she's been so quietly walking behind us. She's probably been hanging on every word I've said.

Once the kids run off and it's just Jack, who's fallen asleep, Diana pauses, retucking the blanket around the harness. "Here's the thing you have to understand about Mark Brader. The confidence, standards, spreadsheets, all of it, it's his safety net. He thrives when things go his way."

"You're making him sound like a tyrant."

"Now hold on. He needs to feel like it's his choice."

"*Project: Find a Wife* is a choice all right."

"Geez Louise, he told you about that? And you didn't run away screaming?"

"He mentioned it before we were friends. I didn't know what to think of it. But knowing him now, it sure fits. Of course Mark would have a spreadsheet for finding a wife. Of course he'd list the candidates and compare them against a list of attributes. Of course! This is why I'm in pure agony over here." I fling my gloved hands in the air, then drop them to my sides with a heavy sigh that sends a puff of white breath into the cold.

My boots crunch against the salted sidewalk as I stomp out a few steps ahead of her, then spin to face her, waiting for her to catch up. "I know exactly what he's looking for, and I don't think it's me. And yet! Diana, he calls me on his lunch break. I've got a front-row seat to his life and dreams and thoughts. He laughs through old musicals with me over the phone. What kind of man does that? He's too—"

"Wow, okay, honey. Take a breath." She takes my elbow and leads us forward. "Let's think about this for a second. He likes you. A lot. That's not in question. Physically, he struggles with claustrophobia. He can't handle being trapped or confined. But I think it goes a little deeper. Why would a boy who grew up in small-town Nebraska pursue a career in Phoenix?"

"You think he hated his hometown?"

"Not necessarily. I think he wanted to prove something to himself. That he was free to make it on his own. His parents are great, but personally I think they smothered him." Diana tilts her head, lips pressed in that half-frown she gets when she's choosing her words carefully.

"What does that mean for me?"

"A couple days of silence shouldn't worry you. But you could check with Cordy. Mark and I are close, but she talks to him every day. She calls him Coach Business, like he's her personal project manager. He was her lifeline for years. She won't take advice from me, but him? He tells her what to do constantly, and she listens." Diana scoffs, shaking her head with a rueful laugh. "Sorry. Now you've got me excited about my sister."

My phone rings with an incoming call. It's Preston.

When I see it, it increases the I-hate-doing-life-today emotions.

"Who's that?"

"Preston is going to ask me out again." I whimper, not knowing how to keep avoiding him.

"Give me that phone. I'll deal with this. Give it." She squares her shoulders and holds me in the mom-stare she has perfected the last ten years until I give up the phone.

"Hello, this is Diana Weston."

She switches the call to the speaker and Preston's voice comes through. "—Nicole's phone?"

"Yes, you did. She's indisposed at the moment."

I cringe. Now he probably thinks I'm sick in the bathroom.

"No worries, I'll call back in a few." Preston is persistent.

"No." Diana hasn't even blinked. "No, you will not. Nicole has said no. She means no."

There's dead air on the other end long enough that I wonder if the call dropped. "Um, I think you might have me confused with someone else?"

"You're Preston Kendrick?"

"That's me."

"Then you're the one."

"I—" Preston blows out a breath.

I'm not breathing. Not moving. Hardly even thinking except *Oh, crap. Oh, crap. Oh, crap.*

"Okay," Preston says, finding his voice. "Nicole has never actually told me no. She is stubborn. And busy, I'll give you that. But I admire her. She's funny, energetic, delightful. I know she's been avoiding me, but if she'd give us a chance at least—"

"Hang on, I need to go. There's an emergency, kid, um,

got to go." Diana ends the call and flings it into the snow as if it turned into a snake. "What the heck, Nickie? Is this true?"

I curl my shoulders in on themselves. "I've made it pretty clear I'm not interested."

"Have you tried, 'Preston, I'm not into you like that. Don't ask me out.' The end."

"I don't want to be rude about it. I still have to work with him, you know," I say while digging my phone out of the snow.

Diana purses her lips, then hunches over with one hand on Jack's back, the other on my shoulder for support.

"Are you okay?"

"Yep," she grunts the word. "Just lovely Braxton Hicks because I'm twenty-nine weeks pregnant and all worked up and stressed out because my best friend doesn't want to hurt anyone's feelings." She unfolds and starts us moving down the sidewalk. "So instead of releasing the poor man, you're going to keep him hoping and string him along like there's still a chance. In turn, you're worried every day because you're overthinking the whole thing. Every time you don't say what you should, you're paying interest instead of the principal. My goodness, Nickie, is this what's going on with you and Mark? How are my favorite people so bad at talking to each other? Have neither one of you been straightforward with what you want? I can't believe this."

She gasps and leans forward again.

I support her through it. "You need to lie down for a bit, mama."

"Don't call me that," she huffs.

"Okay, as soon as you're home, get your feet up. I'm putting you on bedrest for the afternoon. Doctor's orders."

"Sounds great."

We turn toward her front door, and I toss a sled out of our way. "So what should I do about Mark?" I ask tentatively.

"Don't smother him, I guess."

"Or..." I take both of Diana's hands and halt her another moment before she goes into the house.

"The look on your face is frightening. You're plotting a murder or a surprise party, and those two shouldn't be friends."

"Or." I clamp my lips together and wait for Nathan, who's chasing a laughing Lisa down the sidewalk.

"You two coming in?" He swipes up Lisa before she passes the house.

"In a minute. Help Lauren make sandwiches, please." Diana plants her hands on her hips hidden somewhere under her sweater and child. "Or...?"

"Or maybe I should smother him. Why are Cordy and Mark best friends?"

"I don't know. It's never made sense to me because they're so different."

"Because they're honest." Suddenly it all makes sense. It's my *Eureka!* "They're safe. Cordy doesn't hide what she's feeling. Truthfully, I don't think she's capable of it. Mark has standards so high that he only does what he knows is right for him and doesn't care what people think. They trust each other with that honesty. Cordy bares her soul to him because she knows he'll still love her even if he disagrees."

"What are you thinking?"

"What if I Ruth-and-Boaz him?"

Diana sways and bounces her baby wrapped against her chest. It's a subconscious movement that all mothers inherit.

She narrows her eyes in thought. "It could work. But why now? There's no emergency. You met him a month ago."

"I'm off work for the next two days. What would Ruth do? Would Mark run if I surprised him?"

"Surprises are not his favorite. How *Ruth* are you going to *Ruth* him? I forbid you to lay in his bed and cover yourself with his blanket."

"Worked for Ruth."

"I don't care. It's not appropriate. Besides, you can't force him into anything. Isn't that what I've been telling you? It'll explode in your face, and he'll retreat faster than he ever advanced. Talk to his mom, she's been playing this dance his whole adult life. Aunt Sarah says she only calls him once a month so she doesn't scare him."

"But I have to be blunt saying no but not yes?"

"Tell him how you feel, yes! But don't force his hand."

"*Operation Ruth* is a go."

Diana tilts her face to the sky, eyes closed. "Nickie, think about this for half a minute."

"The time for thinking is over." I lift on my toes, ready to move, despite lack of sleep. "I need his hotel address please."

"I can't give you that in good faith unless you promise to be an adult about this. What, you're going to show up and say, 'Pick me?'"

"I have a whole plane ride to figure that out. Okay. I'm off. I'll get the address from Cordy." I start walking backwards.

The disbelief on Diana's face is priceless. "Nickie! This isn't like you at all."

"Yes, it is. It's the real me that's been here the whole time. I'm doing something for myself for once in my life. I'm worried about your cousin. So I'm going to see for myself that he's okay. That's all. A friendly, 'hey, how's the nose?' visit. Don't get yourself all worked up. Go take a nap. I'll be cool. And! What if he needs help? After the racquetball injury, he could be in a lot of pain."

She's still shaking her head. I march back toward her and prop my fists on my hips. "I'll be careful. But I'm not okay sitting here pining for him when he doesn't answer the phone. The thought of being in the same room with him again has my heart beating faster."

"This seems extremely unnecessary." Diana's eyes grow wide like maybe she's resisting the urge to throttle me.

"This is where you're supposed to say, 'Go, my child, and may God be with you.'"

"Why not wait another week until you hear from him? What if he's slammed with work?"

"Go big or go home." I don't fight the thrill of adventure that's building. Why shouldn't I fly across the country on a whim? I have the money. I have the time. Grinning, I spin away and jog down the sidewalk before giving her the chance to talk me out of it.

By the time I reach my house, I've purchased a plane ticket from my phone for this evening.

John's arrived with the grandparents, and Mom and Dad's van is parked in the street. I run up the steps and barrel into the house. "Mom! I need help packing. I think I need a swimsuit. Grandpa! I'm after those chickens. Oh, hey, Dad, can you drop me at the airport? I need to leave here in forty-five minutes."

2 3

———

# MARK

## MONDAY, JANUARY 22

Nickie kicks off her flip-flops and tosses her towel onto the beach. She's wearing cut-off jean shorts and a red tank top. Not a cloud in the sky. Nothing but sun, sand, and waves. Far away from the blizzard of our meeting. Blazing heat envelops me. It's so hot, all I want is to drag her into the water. She waves me onward, but doesn't reach for me. No matter how fast I run, she slips away laughing.

I turn in a half-sleep, disturbed from the dream. My room is dark, with a sliver of a street lamp leaking around my blackout curtains. Sweating, I kick off the covers and tunnel my thoughts back into that place where I'm with Nickie and my face doesn't hurt so much.

My feet sink into the dry sand. The roaring of the ocean covers her laughter. It's been forever and only seconds, yet my feet won't move into the cool water out of the heat. My sluggish legs won't obey. The dream fades, and I sink into oblivion.

The images change, and I'm lounging beside her on a couch. We're in a lodge of some kind with a ceiling so high it disappears into the darkness. Hazy smoke from a fireplace stifles the air and collects in the dim corners of the room. It's very gothic and strange. We're both in winter sweaters. My legs are tangled in an afghan tucked around us.

A whiteboard across the spacious room contrasts with the decor. It lists the names of women I've dated this month. Their names are all crossed out with a single note: *Not Nickie.*

It's cold here despite the fireplace, and I snuggle closer to her. I'm lying with my head in her lap, one arm wrapped over her thighs like my own special teddy bear. Her fingers are cool against my forehead. I shiver in the cold, and she tucks the afghan over my shoulders.

I drift in and out of consciousness as her fingers play gently through my hair and around my ear. She traces around my eyebrows and carefully along the bridge of my nose. With every breath, my nervous system relaxes. Eventually warmth returns.

Her leggings are soft beneath my cheek, and I tighten my arm where it rests on her legs. I love this dream.

"Do you need a pillow?" she asks.

"Um-Mm," I grunt negatively. I glide my hand up the side of her leg, over her hip, and hook it behind her back so I can maneuver her down onto the large couch beside me.

"Mark, what are you doing?" Her voice is laced with humor.

Talking is wasted in dreams like this. It would take too much time to explain how I'm going to kiss her until I wake up and she disappears. I rest my palm on her cheek and lower my mouth to her lips.

They're as soft as I remember. Unlike last time, I have nowhere to go and no audience. I can do anything I want in my dreams. I'm going to kiss her slowly and thoroughly. Except now she's pushing against my bare chest and sliding away. I sigh and rest my head on the warmth left by her. The night is filled with more dreams of the two of us together, but nothing as real as that one.

Staring across the dark room sometime later, I ponder what it'd be like to really sleep next to her. Wake up next to her. I think it would be wonderful. My desire to be with Nicole Brader has grown stronger every day. How was I ever able to walk away from her? I don't think I can keep doing this. Pretending like I'll find someone else that excites me like she does. *God, I'm committed to the work. Please establish my plans.*

The intensity of my dreams sure isn't helping. I blink fully awake. I'm in my bed, not on a gothic couch. My nose is still sore. I stretch to the bedside table and angle my watch to check the time. Three-fifty.

I drag my sorry self out of bed and shut off the alarm that'll go off in a couple minutes, then I toss my earplugs in the drawer. "The first ten minutes is a lie," I mumble my daily encouragement to get up.

You know what's almost as much fun as being an editor? Being the boss of more editors. The past couple weeks we've been busy restructuring our office to function almost entirely remote.

I still keep to my early mornings because I do my best work before eight o'clock, and I check into the office a few times a week—mostly to use our printer. Even Emily gets to work remote for half of the days by switching our office phone to redirect to her cell.

In nothing but a pair of boxer briefs, I stumble with half-lidded eyes into the bathroom. I flip on the light and blink at myself in the mirror. Purple bruises spread from under my eyes, and my nose is discolored and swollen. Not broken but very tender.

Midway through brushing my teeth, I freeze. On the bathroom counter is a pink zippered rectangular bag. N.J.B. is embossed on the side.

One handed, I unzip the bag and dump the contents on the counter. I'm no less confused. Plastic tubes of makeup, lotion, nail polish, toothpaste, tampons...

White foam drips from my mouth as I stare at the foreign objects. I slowly rinse and spit, afraid they might attack if I look away. Someone's been in my room since last night and left their bathroom bag on my counter. A girl someone.

I lean out of the bathroom door, gripping the doorframe on either side and survey my living quarters with only the light from the vanity flooding into the room. There she is.

Nickie's curled on the loveseat wearing my hoodie. Am I awake or still sleeping? I pull back and look at myself in the mirror again. Definitely awake.

I tiptoe over to my intruder. Kneeling, I watch her sleep for a full minute. Because I know I'm in my right mind, there must really be a woman in my room. This feels big somehow. A turning point in our relationship. I've been flirting with Nickie and dancing around my real feelings since she forced out those crocodile tears in an attempt to convince me to take her to the gala. She's somehow turned into the girl of my dreams even when she's not the girl of my long-term vision. How can she be? She has an entire life in Hadley Springs. She is locked in. I would never ask her to leave that to be with me. She'd resent me forever.

Looking into her sleeping face, I consider my options. Option one: Tell her straight that we can't be together. Cut off all communication because it's not fair to be in this limbo relationship we have. Wow, that hurts just thinking about it.

The alternative... the alternative is to rewrite my vision to align with this. Accept that I accidentally fell in love with the wrong girl. No, the right girl. Also scary. That would change everything.

I don't like surprises. They're never as much fun as if you'd been able to plan for it. Planning is half of the fun! The glorious anticipation. The waiting and watching and then the thing happening just like it should. Orchestrating the whole endeavor and working toward an end result is my favorite thing.

The point is, there's a girl on my couch, and I think I'm in love with her when I shouldn't be. What to do with that? I don't know what comes next.

I poke her shoulder, "Hey."

Her eyes pop open. Neither of us move. Then her eyes drift closed again.

"There are tampons in my bathroom."

That opens her eyes, and she smiles. "Good morning."

"Are you named after Grandma Joyce?"

"Mmhmm." Her sleepy eyes crinkle on the edges with a smile.

"Nicole Joyce Brader. Hmmm. N.J.B. I deduce those tampons belong to you."

"Always best to be prepared. Do you think if you keep saying that word it will make it less weird for you?"

"Let's find out. Tampons, tampons, tampons." I try so hard to keep a straight face, but a laugh chokes me with the ridiculousness of what's happening right now. "Tampons." I fall into her and wrap her up against me in a monster hug. "Ahh, what are you doing here?"

"You're not wearing any clothes." Her face is smooshed against my chest.

I squeeze her as hard as I'm allowed. "You broke into my bedroom." I punctuate each word with a little shake. "How did you get in here?"

"You tried to make out with me on your bed."

I tense, holding her flush against me, her breath warm on my skin. Last night's dreams still linger. The truth I won't admit aloud is that she's been in my dreams for weeks. Last night wasn't much different except the part where she was actually in my bed. I ball my fists and ease back to keep from finding out what it really feels like to kiss her senseless.

Pants. Those would be a good idea right about now. I find the strings from the hoodie over her head and pull them until the hood tightens the fabric around her face.

"What are you doing? I can't see," she complains.

"That's the idea. Stay there." First I kiss the tip of her nose, then scuttle away to find clothes. I couldn't care less what she sees of me. I'm not embarrassed about my body, but I'd like to do a lot of other things right now and having layers of clothes between us is prudent.

Dressed in jeans and a sweatshirt, I lean over the counter in my micro kitchen. *Kitchen* is relative. There's a small fridge, a three-foot counter with an extra sink, a toaster oven, and my coffee maker. I blow out a breath and set out two coffee cups.

"Now." I start the coffee and turn on the lights. "You're in my room. You're on my couch. You're wearing my shirt. And I haven't the faintest idea what to do with you. Speak, woman, before I call the cops. I would be angry if I wasn't so happy to see you."

She's sitting up, knees tucked under her chin, and she looks at me sheepishly.

"What? No defense? Is everyone okay? Jeffrey, Joyce, Diana? The kids?"

"Yeah. We're all fine." She smiles.

Everything is so real, I must be awake, but none of this fits her genre. Why doesn't she talk? Nickie always talks.

"I was—" Her lips pull to one side, then the other. Nicole Brader? Tongue tied? "I was worried about you, and I missed you. So I came to see you. That's the meat of it."

I walk carefully toward her with our freshly brewed coffee, sweeping my eyes over her, examining her expression, body language, tone of voice, searching for the truth. The truth of how much more hides beyond her words.

"Why are you smiling like that?" Nickie wraps her hands around her legs and pulls them tighter. "You're like a hungry cat making me feel like a mouse."

"Scoot over." Settled beside her is the only place I want to be. I sit, leaving no room between us, like when we were sandwiched together on the bench outside her house. "Here. Want this?"

"Ohh," she breathes, accepting a mug from me. "Your poor face. I'm so glad it's not broken."

"Same. How'd you get in my room?"

Her eyes brighten with mischief. "Rosita. Last evening I had some trouble at the front desk. I thought I'd be sneaky and flash my ID and they'd think I was your sister or something, but the manager didn't fall for it. I was sulking across the lobby trying to form a new plan when Rosita found me. She recognized me right away. Although I didn't understand half of what she was saying, she got all excited when I asked if she'd show me your room."

"Nobody thought to knock?" Logically, I should be

appalled. I should call the front desk and report this. I should want anything but to hold her.

"Oh, we did! But when you didn't answer, she put her finger to her lips, swiped her card, and walked away."

"That's when you slipped into bed with me like I wouldn't notice."

"It would appear you're a stronger sleeper than Boaz."

## 24

———

# NICKIE

**M**ark's roaring laughter is the last thing I expected. I did the brave, crazy, audacious thing. For me, it's still the middle of the night. I was prepared for his confusion, questions, and—I don't know!—but this laughter I was not ready for.

He wipes his eyes, spasms still shaking his shoulders. "That was reckless of you. Extremely dangerous." He pushes his mug toward me. "Hold this."

Now I'm trapped, holding two cups of burning coffee as he pads across the room and pulls a Bible from a stack of books on his desk. He leans his hip on the side of the desk while flipping through the pages. Mirth shakes him again until he's fully laughing. "Ruth three... Here it is. '*In the middle of the night, something startled the man. He turned*'— and there were tampons in his bathroom! Say whaaat?"

He finds it hilarious, and his laughter's contagious.

Mark sighs on the tail of a laugh. "Oookay. Hang on,

wait for it." He clears his throat. "'*He turned.*' And what's this? '*There was a woman lying at his feet.*' Hmm, how bizarre... Boaz says, '*Who are you?*' Good man. Very important question. Surprise! '*It's Ruth...*' Yada yada. Oh my, he says, '*You've done me a great kindness.*' I don't know about that, Ruth. Bo's more gracious than I am. Look at this, the man says, '*You have not run after the younger men.*'"

Mark dissolves into another fit of laughter, sinking to the floor until he's flat on his back, Bible splayed across his chest.

My Lanta, the man is on happy gas. I love this side of him. I've seen peeks of it, but never the full show. His sense of humor was never in question. The goofiness mixed with the perfect level of professionalism is why he's such a compelling enigma. Tucked away in his private home, he's free of all professional decorum. A man released from restraints.

He rolls his head to look at me. "C'mere, Ruth."

"You're on the floor."

"Yeah, c'mere."

"No, it's not safe. There's a wild man on the loose."

He flips to hands and knees, crawls the few feet where I'm still holding our mugs. "Put those down."

"I think not." I hold them before me like a shield, wondering what he'll do next. They are both so full of black liquid I have to be careful when I move. "Thirsty, sir?"

"Sure." Sitting cross-legged on the floor in front of me he takes the offered mug. Sip, after slow, lazy, sip. He stares at me.

I don't know what to do. I'm here! I fell asleep on the plane instead of writing any kind of speech. I was at his room by nine p.m. and wasn't surprised that he was already asleep. He keeps crazy early hours.

*Extremely dangerous*, he'd said. Yep, that about covers it. His room has one king-sized bed, a desk, loveseat, bathroom, closet, and kitchen area. This is not a luxury hotel. But the bed is huge. I knew I was pushing the line when I got into his bed. Diana would have something to say about it... but I wasn't going to sleep there. Just... WWRD? *Okay?* If the grandmother of King David gets away with it, I thought I'd give it a try. I slipped under the covers and rested against the headboard watching Mark sleep like some kind of stalker.

I'm blushing thinking of it.

Oh, wow. This is terrible. I watched Mark sleep like an obsessed vampire girlfriend.

But then he kicked off his covers and sprawled out on his stomach in nothing but his underwear like he owned the whole bed—which he rents for a monthly rate, but still— there was so much skin and heat and *what am I doing here?* Even through all of that, I was still unable to see his tattoo across his side in the dark room.

Now he's dressed, sitting two feet away, in full light, sipping on his crude-oil, staring me down like he'll extract secrets with his lasers. "Your face is turning pink," he says behind his mug.

"Yeah."

"Watcha thinkin' 'bout?" He speaks slow and sultry like he shares my memories. Why does he make this so hard? I know that he likes me. He knows that I like him. If he doesn't, then he really is off his rocker, and I've fallen for an unstable man.

Fine! I flew here to show him I'm ready for more. No time like the present. "I was thinking about how you laid your head in my lap last night and clung to me like I was your lifeline."

"How about the part where I pulled you down and kissed you. Did that part happen too?"

"You are such a flirt." We're skating around the important parts. We can be adults here. I'm in his hotel room! I'm so afraid he'll bolt if I insist on moving our relationship forward. What if he feels manipulated like I did to him for the gala? Diana already warned me not to corner him. The worst that could happen is he tells me that he's had a good time, but that he's not interested in me. He wouldn't do that... would he?

Would he?

I want to believe his behavior toward me is honest. But how can it be if he's not willing to take the next step and label our relationship? "Mark, I have something to say."

"I'm listening."

I close my eyes on a breath, gathering strength. "I came here because I want you to know that I'm—that I—that I wonder if you'd be willing—could pretend that we're together. If you'd take me on a date and treat me like a girl-friend, and we can see—see what happens."

When I open my eyes, Mark's moved closer. The mug is taken from my hand and then he's dragging me onto his lap on the loveseat. He pulls me firmly against him, my legs hanging off one side, forehead against his neck, and presses my palm flat against his sweatshirt.

After a minute or two, his arms relax. "I think I'm in love with you," he whispers with all the seriousness of a man on trial.

His words knock what little starch that was left out of me for good. My heart stops and then jolts into rhythm as if AED paddles have shocked me off the table. His hand slides under my chin and tilts my face to meet his gaze. Where I expected to see joy, I find concern.

He is tortured. Conflicted. Then in one blissful breath of anticipation, he dips his head until his lips brush against mine. A feather-light touch, testing the temperature, offering me plenty of warning to accept or decline.

I accept, matching his energy.

A peck of a kiss at the door is one thing. That was appreciated.

*That* was oatmeal in the servants' quarters.

This, after a month of deepening friendship and his hesitant confession, is a feast for royalty. It's five-star dining with crystal cups almost too thin to drink from and plates three times the size of the artfully decorated entrée.

Mark and I don't say much else after that kiss. Almost as if we're both afraid to talk about what this means when I leave. Eventually—after a minute or five days—he says, "I have things to do today." *Kiss.* "And I can't let a midwestern blizzard blow through my whole schedule." *Kiss.* "So you'd better go find something to do for the next four hours." *Kiss.*

That is easily accomplished on account of it being four in the morning. "Can I borrow your bed?"

"No."

When I ask why not, he grins like a fool and peppers my face with kisses. It's all very sweet until he calls the front desk and books me a separate room.

So here I am at eight a.m., after a long nap and warm shower, finishing a light breakfast in the lobby, waiting for Mark to reemerge. Next on his bring-your-friend-to-work day is a workout and swim. I'm wearing my swimsuit under my shorts and T-shirt.

I'm wearing shorts. In January! It's fantastic.

After he saunters in with all the authority of an athlete who never skips leg day, we head over to the hotel's excuse of a gym. I make it almost a mile on the treadmill before decreasing my speed to a swift walk. Sweating through everything isn't my first idea of getting a man to move from "I think I love you" to "I'm hopelessly, madly, head-in-the-clouds, forever-yours" in love with me.

He doesn't have any qualms about sweating and runs two miles until his shirt is soaked through. Sweat has never looked so attractive.

I stay on the treadmill while he goes through his regular routine. Squats, dumbbells, push-ups... It's weirdly comfortable being here. We work without talking while listening to his indie rock playlist hooked to the overhead speakers. He's gasping through his fourth set of sit-ups when I call across the room. "Seventeen! Twenty-four! Eight! One hundred five!"

He rolls forward and stands in one fluid motion.

"Uh-oh. You have that hungry cat look about you again."

"Pool. Now." He grabs the back of his shirt and pulls it over his head.

My vision tunnels, and I turn off the machine before I fall on my face. I have the urge to whistle or say something disgustingly cheesy like, "When God made you, he gave himself a high-five and said, 'nailed it!'"

Instead I stumble off the treadmill and guzzle half a bottle of water with my eyes closed. I've seen a man's chest before. *Pfft.* It's no thang.

The pool room has a slight mildew smell mixed with overpowering chlorine. Condensation drips from the discolored ceiling. There's a family with three kids horseplaying in the shallow end. A dad launches a young boy high into the air. The mom lounges on one of the white plastic chairs reading a thick, mass market novel.

I ditch my outer clothes, thankful for the new swimsuit Diana helped me find last summer. I know it matches the exact color of my blue eyes. We take turns rinsing off with the shower in the corner of the room.

Mark steps forward once I'm finished. "Hey, you've got — Hold still."

He uses a dry portion of his shirt to wipe under my eyes. "Thanks, was I a raccoon?"

"A bit. It's better now." Our conversations are normal, but I feel like I'm playing a part. I'm auditioning for Cool Girl #3: woman not bothered standing beside mega-crush while wearing swimsuits. Tony Award nominee right here. Mark's a better actor than I am, or he's not bothered. Hmmm.

I can finally inspect the tattoo on his side that wraps partway onto his back. Tracing the cursive script with my finger, I smile when his abs tighten. "Te-te-le—Move your arm. Te-te-le-stay-ee. What's that?"

"Rhymes with eye. Te-*tel*-*e*-*stai*. It's Greek."

"Tetelestai." I repeat the word slowly. Most men don't show up at a tattoo parlor and slap random words on their sides for no reason. "What's this word mean?"

He brushes a hand through his hair, flinging drops everywhere. At first I think he's not going to answer, but he offers a smile and nods toward the pool. "It's supposed to remind me to relax. Let's cool off, and I'll tell you more."

"Are you a toes-in-first or dive-right-in kind of guy?"

"Will you think less of me if I'm toes-in?" He's walking toward the steps on the end where the family is playing. But he's so close to the edge, *right now,* if I just... He yelps when I push him into the deep end of the pool. In he goes with a huge splash.

He comes up grinning. "If you don't jump in right now. I'm going to chase you down and throw you in."

"Are you threatening, Mr. Brader?"

He's already hoisting himself up the side as he answers. "It's a promise, Dr. Brader." He stalks toward me, and I back away step by step. This is high-school summers and sandy camp rivers. Flashbacks of sunburns and Mountain Dew and blasting Miley Cyrus's "Party in the USA" loud enough that we could belt the lyrics and not be heard.

It's wonderful.

Mark crouches as he stalks, water streaming down his chest. I bump into the end of the room. "Oh, nooo... I'm trapped. Whatever shall I dooo?" With one more step he slaps his palm against the wall by my head with an audible *smack*.

I squeak at the noise and tilt my face to keep my gaze locked with his.

"*Kabedon*," he whispers near my ear, not touching me but caging with both arms on the wall by my face.

"Kaba what?"

"You need to read more books. Man slaps wall by girl's head and leans in. Super romantic."

"I see." My words are barely above a whisper. "I've never been so close to swooning in my entire life."

"Corset too tight?"

"And my terrible shoes. Weak disposition."

"Get in the pool before I lose myself kissing you."

"I choose Option B."

Standing this close, I witness the slight dilation of his pupils. Gooseflesh appears on his forearms beside my face. His breath slows. He leans a millimeter closer.

Then he shoves his arm behind my waist, and I'm slung

over his shoulder. In three steps he's tossed me into the water.

I surface in time to see him grab a towel from the top of a shelf and stride out of the room without stopping when the whole stack tumbles to the floor.

25

———

NICKIE

Mark's picking me up for a lunch date any minute. I didn't pack much, but I like my outfit. Dark jeans, a tank, and an olive cable-knit sweater. I spent time blow-drying and curling my hair into loose waves that fall just past my shoulders.

Staccato knocks at the door catch me mid-swipe of the mascara, and I smear black stripes to my eyebrow. "Dang it." Then louder, "Coming!" I rush to the door, and I'm a swarm of butterflies when I see him. He's upgraded too with hair still damp and artfully mussed. He's in dark slacks, shiny leather shoes, and a gray button-up. "Look what you made me do," I say, pointing to my eye.

"Very fetching." He follows me into the hotel room while I race to the bathroom to scrub the mark off my face. He whistles low. "Nice place you got here."

"Shut up. Where we going? I love this weather by the way, seventy-five degrees in January. I should be in a summer dress."

"I'd love to see you in a summer dress. Let's go shopping." He steps behind me at the sink and hugs me around my waist. "This sweater thing is pretty." His arms release, and he rests his hands on my hips. "You smell nice."

"You're nice." Saying sweet things to each other isn't new. But saying those things while he's casually touching me like a boyfriend is wreaking havoc with my hormones. "Come on, I'm starving."

"Good. Our car will be here at eleven-fifteen." He catches my hand as we leave the room. "I have paperwork to grab at the office. I'll need to work a couple hours this afternoon, but otherwise I'm all yours."

"All mine," I hum. "I like the sound of that."

We have the best nachos I've ever had in all my thirty-two years. Nebraska should be appalled to have duped me this long.

Later, at his office, the euphoria starts to wear thin for the first time. This place is dry and sterile. Gray carpets, gray furniture, white walls. And people that he knows. He drops my hand as we enter.

I take the hint that we're in professional mode now. He's the boss here. No PDA at work. Got it. We pass the front desk where a young woman in a puffed-sleeve blouse eyes me. Mark slows but doesn't stop. "Hey, Emily. This is Nickie Brader."

"Your cousin?" Her hopeful tone shouldn't make me want to inflict bodily harm on her.

"No." Walking backwards, he continues moving away from her. "Do you have the updated manuscript from Haven?"

"Yes." She talks to him, her expression immediately possessive.

I lift a hand and silently open my mouth in a *hi*.

"Good. Print that for me, please. I'll take it home." Mark saunters down the hallway without explaining anything to Emily. His office is at the end of the hall, a corner room with glass walls and a view of the street below. At first glance I'm impressed until I see it's a back alley with a dumpster... not inspiring. There are shades on every wall pushed open all the way.

"Make yourself comfortable. This might take an hour or more. I have a call with a new author. I'll be across the hall in the conference room. You going to be okay?" He fidgets with his hands in his pockets. "Sorry, I guess I could have left you at the hotel."

"It's fine. I'm the one who surprised you. I'm just happy to be here."

"Okay. Hang tight."

And I do. I call Grandpa and make sure he's had breakfast and lunch. I text Diana that Mark is healthy and happy. With nothing else to occupy my mind, I put the phone down and take inventory of Mr. Brader, Editor-in-Chief's office.

It is so... empty. I fiddle with papers on the desk and without meaning to, I start reading a handwritten note. The pen is still lying on the page.

*If we had only one night, Anita, I would spend it with you. The world and all its sorrow would disappear. I'd be safe with you. My heart beats in time with yours. Let our souls entwine as we fall into oblivion together.*

What the crap is this? Who is Anita? I bet everyone hates her. She probably doesn't have any friends because she's a terrible person. I read the note again, twice, three times. This isn't even good writing. I mean, sure, if you knew the world was gonna crumble, go spend it with your people. Souls entwined as we fall into oblivion? That's messed up.

"That didn't take so long." Mark breezes through the door.

I drop the note, startled.

"You ready to go?"

"Who's Anita?" Gosh, I sound like a possessive girl-friend. I cringe at the sharp zing that was more accusation than question. Smile. Try again with a tone that's just curious—not crazy. "I stumbled upon this note, so I was wondering who-o-o Anita is. No reason. Juuust curious."

"Oho, you're not—" He steps forward. "—jealous. Are you?"

"Of course not. *Psh.*" I take the paper and hold it over the trash can. "Why would I be jealous? It's not like this is your handwriting from your own pen at your desk." The paper floats to the trash, but as paper does, it swooshes away and slides across the industrial carpet to Mark's feet.

"Anita." Mark steps on the page. "Is a character in a client's book. I'm going to draft a new declaration for her, but haven't finished."

"I knew it! Of course she's not a real— Hey, what are you doing? Why are you—"

"You're territorial." Mark's hands cup my face, and he has a triumphant look about him. "If that's how you feel about Anita, tell me what you really think of... say, Trisha... Abigail?"

I pinch my lips together and shake my head. I refuse to slander women I haven't met. Er, or anyone. Especially after my embarrassing little outburst. I've already stuck my neck out today. Aren't I here, in his arms? Me. Not anyone else.

My breath stalls as Mark curves around me and presses

a hot kiss to my neck, branding me with a searing iron. "Mark! We're in your office."

He lays a line of little kisses up the side of my neck. "I can see your heartbeat pulsing in this vein." He kisses a spot above my collarbone. "Right here. And you smell like ice cream or vanilla cookies."

"Emily might be watching," I murmur, but I have zero power to retreat as his hand moves across my shoulder and down my arm.

He takes my balled fist and kisses the back of my fingers.

"I feel hogtied, shanghaied, and bamboozled. Don't you care what they think of you?"

"Sure." Mark opens my fist one finger at a time and presses my hand against his side. The thin cotton of his dress shirt is a poor barrier from the radiating skin beneath. "You're so beautiful, Nicole. And delicious."

The gold flecks in his brown eyes lure me closer. I'm a starving traveler who's found a feast inside a castle. There's a table spread with everything I've ever wanted and the guard at the door simply nods and gestures for me to help myself. Dare I? Is it really for me?

I didn't realize how hungry I was until Mark came along. Didn't realize how much I'd neglected my own desires and dreams. I've been doing the next right thing for so many years, I hadn't asked if it was *my* right thing. Of course, I have no regrets about caring for my grandparents. I would do it all over again to keep them with family and out of nursing homes, but *this*. This, right now, with Mark, has substance in it I didn't know existed.

The Nickie of years past who wanted to *do things* and travel and be wild and fun is still here. The work I've accomplished is good and has changed me too. I'm braver and know my own strengths. I save lives! I've attended the births of over a hundred babies. That is amazing. But in those stories I'm the sideshow. I'm the helper. At the end of those days I still go home and sleep in a room by myself.

Ten years ago I would have been embarrassed, too busy perhaps, or even distracted memorizing flashcards for a test to initiate a kiss with a man in his glass-walled office. I never considered I could be a professional and a woman. I didn't fly across the country to worry about what someone might think of me. Of us. The time for thinking is over.

I wrinkle the front of Mark's shirt in a tight grip and pull him back down as I rise on my toes to settle a kiss against his lips.

His mouth lifts into a smile against my kiss, and his hand covers my hip, turns us, and presses me the last few inches to the glass wall.

He holds me upright because without his support I'd be a puddle on his office floor. "I've always fantasized about doing that." His gaze darts over my shoulder. "You probably don't want to look, but a few people have definitely noticed." He lifts his hand in a cocky two-fingered wave at someone behind me.

"Mark, I'm afraid."

"Nah, they'll get over—"

"Excuse me." Emily is suddenly in the room. "I see you're very busy with your *friend*, but can I talk to you for a minute? Alone?"

# 26

## MARK



T*his had better be important* is what I want to snap at Emily like some kind of billionaire executive. I straighten away from Nickie as she slides from under my arm until she's partway behind me.

Emily's gaze roves between Nickie and me, and I know she's trying to unravel who this is. My blood is still rushing and emotions are all over the place. I pause a moment so I don't lash out. I'm not required to ask Emily's permission to bring people into my office.

I squeeze Nickie's hand and meet Emily's glare. I've seen her upset plenty of times through the years. Usually it's at someone else, and she's indignant and ranting to me about it. She and I have worked very well together. I let her talk, tell her what to do, and we move on.

"What do you need?" I find my voice. "We were on our way out. My car's on its way."

"Bethany and I were texting just now. She hasn't told

me that you've canceled." She's tapping the pen against her skirt.

That's right. Bethany was a friend of Emily's. We're going out tomorrow night. I have a reservation for us at a Brazilian restaurant in Scottsdale.

I look at Nickie. She says nothing. Her poker face is cleared of emotion.

*God, please, I'm ready for the proof.* She was clearly jealous over a fictitious Anita, but she's never tried to persuade me from seeing other women. I'm desperate for her to claim me for more than an impulsive visit.

"I have a date tomorrow." I watch Nickie's expression, and there's not a flicker of tension.

Her right shoulder barely lifts in a shrug. The faintest smile—or is it a grimace?—lifts the corner of her lips. "Okay."

"Okay?" It's the kill shot to the chest. After all we've shared today, she says, *okay* about me going with someone else. Well, *okay*, then. Why did she even come if she's not willing to take the next step?

I ball my hands then open them with effort.

"Okay." She walks to the desk and slings her leather crossbody bag over her shoulder. Are her movements more stiff than normal? Is she watching the floor as we make our way down the hallway because she's embarrassed to be caught kissing me, or is she upset I'm going out with Bethany?

"What do you want for dinner?" I pass the elevator and open the door to the stairs. I pause with my hand on the door. "You can take the elevator if you want."

"This is fine. Exercise is healthy, right?"

"Sure." Twelve stories of roundabouts is a great workout.

She didn't question it when we climbed the stairs. It wasn't until the sixth floor that I even remembered the elevator option for her. I haven't used the elevator here in six years, not about to start today when it feels like I'm holding my anxiety in check with a ripped cardboard box and masking tape.

"Mark, I–I'm sorry for showing up unannounced." Her foot slips on a step, and I catch her elbow.

"It's fine." I release her and continue down another flight, outpacing her again. "I had fun. What do you want to eat?"

"Um, anything you want. I'm not very hungry actually. What would you eat if you were here alone?"

"Tuna melt in the toaster oven." I push out a labored breath. The walls are encroaching. The white concrete cinder blocks are better than the box of the elevator, but it's still suffocating. "Can I meet you at the bottom?"

"Yeah, go ahead."

Round and around I go, my shoes barely making contact with the steps, until I burst out of the emergency exit into the sun, gasping for air. I'm out. I'm free.

I pace around the corner and wave at the black car waiting at the curb.

I jog to the car and let him know it'll be a couple minutes. My breath's coming too fast, and I fight the familiar twinges of a full-on attack. I press my fingers to my throat and check my pulse. "Shut it down, Mark."

I'm safe. I'm in control. I'm not stuck. I don't have to do anything I don't want to do. I want to be a man of my word. I have unlimited potential. Unlimited abundance. *Lord, I commit my days to you, establish the work of my hands.*

I'm sitting on the curb, trying to get my heart rate under control when my phone chimes.

Nickie: Didn't you need the manuscript
from Emily? I'm going back to grab it.

I stare at the screen until my eyes burn then text back.

Mark: Thank you.

*In*, two, three, four. *Hold*, two, three, four. *Out*, two, three, four. *Hold*, two, three, four. I repeat the box breathing until Nickie comes out the front door, and I've got my heart beating a normal rhythm. A soft breeze lifts the hair off her shoulder. She must have taken the elevator down. She walks closer, her face unreadable, a paper box against her side.

*God, she's perfect. Why is she here?*

I meet her halfway and offer my hand.

She slips hers in mine with a closed-mouthed smile.

I ask the driver to take us through a drive-thru for a couple of sub sandwiches.

"Want to walk around outside for a while? There are a ton of trails around the city. Or museums? I don't know where to take you. They've got art studios, botanical gardens. Malls?"

She squeezes my hand that I haven't released. "I just want to be with you. Anywhere is fine."

Although she's sitting beside me, our sides touching—legs, hips, arms, hands—I feel we've lost the path. We're on the edge of a cliff and there's no safe way to get down. I might be able to fix it with words and promises. Instead, anger surges. I don't want to fight with her. Especially not in the backseat of a car.

The evening moves along quickly. We walk around a park, sit on a bench and feed the geese. We laugh at a yappy Pomeranian dragging his leash as he dashes through the flock of aggressive birds. It's mostly good, but neither of us address the plot hole. Probably because we don't know how.

We're standing beside a picturesque pond on a hard-packed dirt path. Well, she's standing, I'm fidgeting on the trail, kicking rocks and looking for smooth skipping stones. "What time is your flight?"

She tosses a pebble in the water. "Seven in the morning. I know you'll need to work, so we can say good-bye tonight."

I press my hand against my chest. The extra tightness hasn't released since we left the office. I will not have a panic attack today. I refuse. I check my watch. We could head home soon.

My heart picks that moment to jackhammer against my sternum. With no warning, the pressure that's been building all day, finally explodes. My lungs freak out. This time I know I can't breathe my way out of it. I can't breathe at all.

# MARK



"Mark, are you okay? You're so pale your bruises stand out like a kid took a paint set to your face."

"I'm fine." My hands tingle—half asleep. I take another step and my knee gives, causing me to stumble. I'm gonna die. I'm gonna pass out, fall in the lake, and drown. *God, just take it. Take it. Take it.*

"Here's a bench, let's sit." She takes my elbow and pushes me to sit. Her fingers press the side of my wrist, and she looks at her watch, lips moving as she counts. "Your pulse is pushing one-forty. What's going on?"

I slouch on the bench with my arms resting on each side of me. Short empty breaths through my mouth. Chest pain intensifies.

"Mark, talk to me. Look at me." Nickie moves in front of me. With gentle pressure she opens one of my eyes and then the other. "Dilated pupils," she mumbles. "Racing heart. Shallow breaths."

I wrench my face from her hands and turn away as my eyes burn and tears spill down my cheek.

She takes my hand and holds it between hers. "Mark, has this happened before?"

"It's not—a heart attack." I gasp the words, afraid I'll weep like an infant if I can't get it together.

"I should hope not. You're twenty-nine!"

"Meds are at home." Too far away to matter. We're half an hour from home—if a car came now. I can't get into an inclosed vehicle on the edge of a mental breakdown. It would kill me for sure.

"For this? How often does this happen?"

I curl over myself, overwhelmed by the pain. A javelin punctures my heart.

It's not what it seems. It's not real. It's not a heart attack.

I know I'm not dying because the last two times I went to the emergency room, they confirmed it wasn't a heart problem. It's not my heart, I'm a pathetic man who can't keep control of his mind.

*Oh, God, I'm going to die. Please take me home. Let me leave and be done with this. It hurts so much.*

"I think you're having a panic attack."

My jaw clenches and shoulders convulse with each gasping breath.

"Ohhh, Mark, honey." Nickie stands between my knees and hugs my head against her stomach. "Breathe, honey, keep breathing."

I press my palms to her back and drag her closer.

"You're allowed to cry, Mark. It doesn't make you stronger to keep it inside. Everyone needs a good cry every now and then. I make a habit of it—once a month on the dot whether I need it or not." Her fingers dig into my hair, nails scratching along my scalp in circles.

Big gulping lungfuls of air aren't enough to fill the crevice that's cracking me open.

"Mark, I'm going to keep talking. Your job is to keep breathing. Let it pass through. Hold me as tight as you need. I promise I'm good for it. Listen to me and believe that you are safe. Lord Jesus, protect and shelter Mark. Send Your Spirit to fill him up to bursting with hope and the power to understand Your love." She moves one hand to my back and rubs down one side and up the other.

I know I've sweated through my dress shirt, but it doesn't seem to bother her. Her touch continues, and her voice and her words flow around me.

Who knows how much time has passed when I eventually find the band around my chest has unlocked. I can breathe without shuddering. My arms tremble as they're clasped together behind her back.

Nickie's hugging my head and gently rocking side to side. She's humming, the way a person does when they're not aware.

Nobody else knows this flaw of mine. The claustrophobia is something I've had since childhood after I fell out of a tree and had to spend a week in the hospital with my leg in a sling. Claustrophobia is manageable with pre-planning and anxiety meds before flights. These attacks are different. And now, I live in the fear of never knowing when my mind's going to usurp control and cripple my body. The best I can do is keep everything in order. Control what I can. Let go of the rest.

"I ordered a car a little while ago." Nickie talks softly. "Take all the time you need. It's waiting by the curb whenever you're ready."

I give her a squeeze, then stand on weak legs and turn away. I can't make myself look at her. My worst has been yanked out of my chest and thrown at her feet. I don't want to witness any pity or compassion—at best—disgust or indifference at worst.

When we get home, I'm not brave enough to let go of her hand. She follows me without words when I open the door. Once we're in my room I don't know what to do.

I told her I loved her this morning.

"Want to watch a movie?" Her voice is far away through a tunnel.

"Whatever you want. I need to lie down."

"I'll get you some water. Maybe less coffee for you moving forward? Caffeine can sometimes make anxiety worse with—"

"I don't need a doctor. Forget it, Nickie. I don't. Need. A doctor."

"Right. Sorry, I'll head back to my room. Let you get some rest, I'm sure you're exhausted after—"

"Sure." I take off one shoe and then the other. Each movement deliberate. Calm. Then I pitch the shoe against the wall with all the strength left in me. A burst of a tantrum that I wish would break something I can fix. It didn't. All it did was unscrew the cap of my anger.

The anger that won't stay quiet anymore. "Sure, Nickie. Tuck your tail and go on back home." I know I shouldn't raise my voice. Yet, it's like the words won't be stopped. "Let me bleed all over you. Rip my heart out and stomp on it. Please, go back to Nebraska. That's perfect. Freaking perfect."

She stands with a hand on the doorknob, expressionless. I wish she would yell or cry. Anything but her aloof mask.

"Why did you come? To torture me? Show me what I can't have? Show me what will never be mine? You're here to remind me of your close-knit family and your Grandpa, who's still alive? Your brother who'd give anything for you? Your community who loves you and the ground you walk on. Go back to that."

I know I need to stop. Reel it in. Wait, breathe, pray.

But I don't.

I let it keep spilling out. A fountain of filth. A wicked part of me wants to humiliate her, as if that will make me less pathetic. "It's only ever been me. I give and I work and give and work and at the end of the day, what do I have to show for it? A rewarding job with lousy pay, a shabby hotel, but you know, it works for me. I'm committed to the work. It's all mine. It's fine if you don't want a part of this, but it'd be nice if you'd say something honest for once and quit playing with me. Is that *okay* with you? Is this what you imagined when you bewitched me in front of my nephews?"

Nickie's knuckles turn white as she clutches the strap of her purse. She's staring at the wall over my shoulder.

I let the silence envelop us. It sinks like a sticky cloud.

When it's clear she's not going to say anything, I keep going. "Was your plan simply to sabotage mine? Well, congratulations! I want a wife and a family. I want more than this. So, I'm going to get it. It's not Trisha or Abigail." I dig my phone out of my pocket and plug it in on the desk. My hands fumble with the cord. "And it's not going to be Bethany because she's already canceled. Emily probably gossiped to her about us."

Nickie's lip trembles while her fist runs up and down the leather strap across her chest.

"What did you expect out of this trip?"

She doesn't move. Her silence is hard to understand. I've probably scared her. I'm the bad guy.

I sink to the edge of the bed, the fight slipping through me.

"You know what I thought?" My voice is controlled and soft. "I thought maybe you were serious about us. Was it all a game to you?" I lean forward and hang my head.

The door clicks quietly shut, and I know she's gone.

Her coffee mug from this morning sits on the floor by the couch. Right where I left it before I confessed my feelings. Rosita makes my bed and cleans my bathroom, but she doesn't do the dishes.

I fall into bed. Not caring that it's barely seven p.m., I curl on my side and let myself be angry at everyone.

Tomorrow Nickie will return to Hadley Springs.

And me? I'll be *okay*.

2 8

———

MARK

FOR KING AND COUNTRY—BURN THE SHIPS

An unrighteous harpsichord snaps me out of the depths of sleep. It's ten p.m. My phone vibrates along the top of the desk along with the shrill ringtone. It's Nathan. I close my eyes and groan, aware I've been tattled on.

I swipe to answer and don't bother with a greeting. "I know. I went too far."

"Uncle Mark?" It's Lauren's tender voice. She always sounds even younger on the phone.

I click on the lamp to try to wake up my brain. "Hey, little girl. Isn't it past your bedtime? Everything okay?"

"Not really. Um, I borrowed Dad's phone to call you."

"I noticed. What's up?" I rotate my arm, stiff from sleeping in a ball.

"I was in Mom's room when Nickie called, and I think they forgot I was in there because she didn't tell me to leave. But Nickie was crying a lot."

So I was tattled on. I make my way to the filter for a glass of water. "Yeah, I can't do anything about that."

"But isn't she in Phoenix with you?"

"She's in Phoenix," I answer with a sigh. "What'd she say?"

"A lot of stuff."

"Like?"

"Well, she said you were really happy when you woke up and she was there. Then Mom got mad and kinda yelled at her about being in your room, then Nickie said she loves you, which we're like 'duh,' and then she said—"

"She said she loved me?" Water fills and overflows my cup.

"Yeah, but we already know that, and then she said, 'We must have crossed the streams because it doesn't make sense.' And when I asked what 'crossed the streams' means, Mom screamed like I was a spider. Hello, I've been here the whole time! But then she kicked me out of her room, and didn't tell me what that means."

"Crossed the streams is from a movie you haven't seen."

"But what is it?"

"It's bad. Things blow up." I chug the whole cup. "Except at the end it's the thing that saves the day."

"Uncle Mark, she's really upset, and you sound super sad. Why don't you go fix it?"

"Lauren, I appreciate you calling me." I unbutton my wrinkled dress shirt with one hand. "You're a good friend. But I can't do what you're asking me."

"Mark can do anything through Christ who gives us strength, so you don't get to sit there and spout lies about *can't*."

"Who taught you to be so bossy? This isn't as simple as math, kid." Now I'm defending myself against a ten-year-old. Cool, cool. It would be funny if it were happening to anyone else.

"Uncle Mark, now you listen to me." Whoa, little Lauren sounds a lot like her mom all of a sudden. "The whole reason Nickie went down there was because she's mad you're dating other girls. I heard her say it. She totally misses you like every day. It's all she talks about! So if she loves you, and you love her, why is she crying to Mom like everything is finished?"

Everything is finished. The truth rockets out of the void and whacks me upside the head. *Tetelestai. It is finished.* I had the word seared into my side because I have the habit of missing the forest for the trees.

"Tetelestai," I whisper. The word Jesus cried before he died. It's finished. The end. Debt paid. Charges dropped. Released and walking free. I lost track again, worrying so much over today, my work, the plans, when it's already finished.

"What?"

"Earth sucks, Lauren, but the end of the story's already been written."

"What?"

"It's an HEA. The plot gets tricky, MCs admit defeat, sometimes it feels like the antagonist will win, but nothing can pull us out of the book because the end is written."

Lauren huffs. "What are you talking about? What's an HEA?"

"Nothing. I was thinking of Granddad. I'm sorry you never met him. He always reminded me that I was complete. Plans are good, but who directs our steps?"

"Uncle Mark, I really don't know what you're saying."

"You're the best, Lauren. Thanks for calling. I'm sorry she's crying."

"Are you going to *fix* it?" She's back to being ten with a hundred percent sass.

My nose spikes with unshed tears, and I let the urge deepen for once, knowing that Lauren can't see. "I'm going to try."

"There is no try. Do or do not."

I chuckle. "Thanks, Yoda. I love you. Go on to bed now before you get in trouble."

## 29

─────

# NICKIE

### TUESDAY, JANUARY 23

My reflection in the airport bathroom would make the cover of a haunting thriller. Eyes bloodshot. Flat, stringy hair. Wan complexion—except for the purple under my eyes dark enough to pass for bruises.

Bruises. Like Mark's face this week, still healing from his racquetball accident. The injury should have removed some of my attraction to him. If I was infatuated with his good looks, a swollen nose and black eyes should have cured that.

It didn't. If anything, desire increased at his ruggedness. His personality blazed through with the same strength as before. How can I leave after what happened last night? But I don't know what else to do to show him how I feel about him.

I swipe through pictures from yesterday and pause at one that has me both smiling and hurting. Mark is mid-laughter across the table with our huge plate of nachos. He's holding a chip over the plate, salsa dripping because he was laughing too hard to take another bite. The shot is blurry because he couldn't sit still. I don't even remember the joke. He was foot stomping, shoulders shaking, mouth open laughing. Pure joy radiates from him.

My heart misses him already. I don't know how tears can still be produced after last night. For sure I would have bought out the whole factory, but as I stare at the alien in the mirror beneath these awful fluorescent lights, the shimmer gathers into a pool that rushes over my makeup-free lashes.

An airport custodian backs out of the stall behind me. I dip my face and run cool water over my hands. She's mopping the floor around me, and I step aside to the air blower. My hands dip into the vortex and the sound fills the otherwise empty bathroom when she appears at my elbow.

She places a small card on the counter and slides it a couple inches toward me. "If you need help," she whispers.

I look at the card, confusion dipping my eyebrows. There's a number printed on the scrap of cardstock and nothing else. I've seen this number before. On the inside of bathroom stalls, gas stations, at my clinic... It's the number for the national human trafficking hotline.

The woman has already exited the bathroom by the time I look up. I'm appalled. I look so wretched that someone thinks I might need saving. On the other hand, she's done no harm if she's wrong. Perhaps she hands out the card to any woman standing alone. I imagine she comes across all sorts of people in this bathroom.

I swallow a lump in my throat and pull my suitcase toward security.

Not fifteen feet from the bathrooms, Mark Brader is a new art fixture in the large concourse. It takes me a minute to process the words on the sign he's holding: "I would like to buy Naomi's property."

People mostly ignore him. City people don't pay attention to what doesn't concern them. Mark's not bothered by the crowd that's streaming around him. If he tried this in Hadley Springs, word would be across town in five minutes and his picture would be in the town's Facebook group within the hour and the local paper the next week.

He smiles when I step forward. He keeps the sign up until I'm standing three feet in front of him.

"You would like to buy Naomi's property?" I try to sound unaffected.

He nods. "Please."

"You know her property comes with a desperate woman willing to try anything to get Boaz's attention."

"I was counting on it."

"What will you do with this property? You live in a hotel. Taking care of a bit of land may not be very efficient."

"Nor cheap. Snow removal is more than my phone bill."

"That was you? This whole time? You've been taking care of me *this whole time!*" My voice screeches beyond our bubble and people turn to look at us. Abashed, I lower my voice. "And the donut deliveries?"

"Paid Landon to drop them off."

"Mark, my heart can't take it. What are you doing?"

"Let's cross the streams, Dr. Brader."

The noise of the airport is a clacking machine. Snippets of distinct voices blend into indistinguishable chatter. "Lauren called you."

He nods.

"Lauren called you, and now you're quoting *Ghostbusters.* What is even happening? Pinch me." I stick out my arm and yelp when he obeys. "Explain it to me with crayons. Use small words."

"I was wretched last night. I'm sorry. I have no excuse."

"I forgive you. Your shoe was the only casualty, and I think it's probably fine." I look anywhere but his earnest face. "Um, Diana thinks I haven't been as clear as I meant to be. I think it's wrong for me to feel possessive, and I never wanted you to think I was—" Sniffing, I unzip my purse for another tissue. "I didn't want you to think I was telling you what to do."

When I pull out a tissue from the package, it bursts open and flutters of white cotton scatter around my feet. "Ugh, what I'm trying to say is that I really hate that you were dating other people. Okay? I hate them all, and I'm a jealous, nasty person, but I wanted you to see me. To really see me, and I didn't want you to feel like I'd yanked you around after what I did to you for the gala."

Mark's gaze is locked on my face, and it's so intense and serious, I can't keep looking at him.

I kneel and gather the mess I've made while still talking. "But I figured if I could just be so happy and such a good friend, and do my best to be content, that you would find what you wanted whether it was me or someone else." I stand, a ball of white fluff held in both hands. "But I really want it to be me. So I came to ask if you'd put my name on your list." I look at the ceiling, so embarrassed to be saying all of this. "And cross off the other names. Just me. So when you had another date already scheduled, I was back to waiting in line for you to figure out what you wanted."

"So you said, 'okay.'" Mark slowly shakes his head. "That word tore me apart. I needed one sign that you'd claim me."

"I literally crawled into your bed as Ruth."

"Extremely dangerous, by the way. But why didn't you fight for me in front of Emily? Gosh, this is hard to admit. I felt so pathetic yesterday."

I chew my bottom lip, completely aware of all the people streaming around us and not knowing what to do with the wrinkled tissues in my hands. "If I knew you'd appreciate it, I'd fight all of them for you. Maybe give me a few weeks to train."

Mark takes the tissues and shoves them into my open purse. "So you know at the end of *The Music Man*, everyone's chasing Harold and his world's about to implode, but he can't leave because he knows Marian is the one?"

"I'm familiar."

"How about in *Calamity Jane* when she realizes her true feelings then gallops off after the stage coach to set everything to rights?"

"I know the story."

"Great, so in *My Fair Lady*, Eliza should not have come back after Henry Higgins was such a beast, but she does anyway because she loves him. Despite his faults and his outbursts and his peculiar habits, she loves him. The man's been alone for so long, he has a certain way of doing things. He needs time to realize that the thing he needs, this person who completes him, has been standing in front of him. They've gotten to know each other and there's trust and even intimacy between them even though he lives half a country away, Henry's going to figure out a way to make it work because—he's grown accustomed to the girl from Nebraska and nothing makes sense without her. Even when he's rude and doesn't understand how amazing she is. She is this beautiful and unexpected gift that fell into his life before he had the chance to work for it."

There's nothing flippant or casual in his expression—

just that earnest way about Mark that convinces me to believe everything he says.

"Are we still talking about musicals?"

"I love you, Nickie. So, I'm simply asking if you want to do life with me."

Nodding, I wipe salt water from my face with a fresh tissue. "I love you so much, Mark, I can't stand it. But you had to do this when I'm all weeping and ugly?"

Mark drops his sign and tries to step closer. My suitcase blocks his way, and he kicks it to the side. "Get over here, woman. There's no pool to throw you in, no blizzard to confuse me. I'm about to kiss you into oblivion."

And that's exactly what he does.

A whistle from someone walking around us makes me laugh, but I don't stop. Let them look! Kissing Mark is unfairly consuming. I taste his bottom lip and a groan emanates from the back of his throat. I would gladly have missed my flight—for a fact—if it were all up to me.

Mark keeps me on schedule though. Before I drown in his love, he pushes me away, out of breath. "You have to go." He checks his watch. "It's five-thirty. Get in line, so you're not late."

"Oh man, we can't do the airport scene where I give up everything to be with you right now?"

"Heck, no." He takes my suitcase and tugs me toward the line. "Don't be ridiculous. Your family needs you, and you have sick people to help. I have books to save yet today, and then I'll figure out what to do." One step before I enter the queue he pulls me aside. "I'm done with the project, okay? *Tetelestai*. It's finished. It's you. It's been you from the beginning."

# MARK

---

## TUESDAY, FEBRUARY 14



"**D**on't touch that." I block Grandpa Jeffrey from pressing another button on the fancy touch-screen radio. "It took us fifteen minutes to get it back to English last time."

"Your car has more buttons than my oven." Grandpa presses another one on the ceiling. "What's this one do?"

I lower my binoculars as the sunroof quietly retracts in my brand-new-to-me 2018 Porsche Macan.

"Ope, that's not what we want." He mashes a few more buttons trying to close the sunroof. As the roof continues to open, he manages to turn on the dome lights and the individual reading lights. "Well, tarnation," he grumbles when he fully opens the sunroof screen and melted snow drips on his head.

"Hold these." I pass him the binoculars and close the roof. "Now focus, Jeffrey. Let's go over the plan again."

"Alright..." He holds the binoculars against his thick

glasses, watching his daughter's house where Nickie has just gone inside to pick up Joyce from her mom's daycare. "When she opens the door. You're going to drive to the house. Hand her the flowers, give your speech, probably smooch a little."

"And what are you going to do?"

"I'm going to take pictures with your phone."

"Perfect, now if—"

*Call from Nickie Brader* lights the screen as a shrill ring-tone replaces our music. Before I intercept, Grandpa presses the green button. Normally she doesn't call me until after four! This was not supposed to happen.

"Hey, honey, what's up?" I say quickly, while slicing a finger over my throat to remind Grandpa not to speak.

"Mark, do you have a minute?"

"Uhhh, no, not really. Now's not a good time. Sorry, can I call you back in a little bit?"

"Oh." She sounds defeated, and I immediately feel bad.

"I mean, I have a little time. Is something going on?"

"No," she says with a sigh. "I'm picking up Grandma from Mom's, and it made me miss you so much. With it being Valentine's Day and everything, I feel rotten we're so far apart."

Grandpa sneezes into his elbow then looks at me with wide eyes.

"Mark, are you okay? That was really loud!"

"Yeah, um, I need to go. Gotta find a..."

Grandpa is trying to tell me something, mouthing whole sentences and waving his hands around.

"Um, Nickie, I'm kind of with someone right now. I—"

"Mark, are you coming?" Grandpa speaks in a terrible falsetto.

I frantically hit the end-call button.

"Jeffrey!" His guilty face is so classic I start laughing mid-lecture. "You're fired! You're the worst stakeout partner in history." Resting my head on the back of my tan leather seat, I rub my hands over my face. "Okay, new rule. Don't touch anything. Here." I pass him the disgusting gas-station coffee in a paper cup. "Drink this."

"There they are." He points down the block as Nickie helps Joyce through the door. "Let's go, partner. Go, go, go!"

I slowly ease to the house and park behind John's car that Nickie still borrows.

The moment she sees me through the windshield, her face morphs into shock, then delight. I'm out the door and on my way to wrapping her in my arms when a chorus of screaming children alert me to the parade a moment before Lance, Leo, and Landon barrel into me. I'm knocked off balance and fall into the melting pile of snow in the yard.

"Boys! Really? Get off. These are my nice clothes." I can't stay upset for long when everyone is smiling and laughing.

"Marky Mark!" Cordy offers a hand to help me up. "What are you doing here? Gilbert and I are walking the kids downtown for pizza. You're a pretty fun bonus."

I can't get a word out between the shouts of the kids, helping Lisa from where she's fallen, and a string of new questions from Cordy. Glancing at Nickie, my heart settles. She's standing with Joyce still on her arm, smiling with a love I feel from here.

Gilbert takes Joyce's other arm and frees Nickie. Ignoring the rabble around us, she falls into my open arms.

Finally, this is home. I hold her with my eyes closed and cheek pressed against her hair. This is all I've wanted.

The beep of a horn gets our attention, and Nickie and I both turn toward the noise. "Mr. Brader! Congratulations." My realtor slows to a stop in the street. "The seller accepted your offer. I have the paperwork here if you want to sign now."

I shake my head, astounded. "I'll call you tomorrow."

Nickie releases her hold, but stays in my arms. "Mark, what's going on?"

"Well, it seems your crazy town has its own agenda for this day. I was going to surprise you. Lakeview Publishing is now completely remote. I have flowers and tickets to a musical in Omaha for tonight. I was hoping to drive us in my fancy new car. But at this rate, I think I'd better just give you the playbook."

Nickie sucks in her bottom lip as tears spill over her cheeks. "You're really here?"

"Please tell me these are happy tears?"

She gasps at something behind me. "He was in on it too?"

Grandpa makes his way around my car with a red binder in hand. "Here, son. You forgot your notes."

"Perfect." I take the binder and pass it to Nickie, but I don't release it. "I'd like to say that I'm flexible, but in reality, you know variables are hard for me. I've been working on a new plan. Come on now, don't look so scared." I finally release my hold and let her take it.

She opens the cover and scoffs. "*Project: Nickie.* Oh, please, don't tell me you've been plotting how—" Her eyebrows jump, and she looks at me with her mouth open. "You have a list of important dates."

Suddenly she's flipping pages and skimming each entry. I chuckle each time she gasps. "You're proposing in

September. Engagement party in October. Wedding in November!" The pitch of her voice rises with each exclamation. "You even scripted what you'll say when—" She smacks it shut and pushes the binder against my chest as one hand flies to her mouth. "Yes," she yells. "To all of it. Yes and yes."

"Woohoo!" Cordy bounces over and squishes us in a quick hug amid the dancing and shouting ring of kids then leaves us to kiss Gilbert.

"I love you." I lean into Nickie and hope she can hear me. "You're more amazing than anything I could have planned. I know I'm a lot to handle. I'm a little cracked. I need structure, or I fall to pieces and—"

Nickie's fingers slide up my neck and into my hair. She pulls me into a kiss that is as grounding as it is electric. "I am so madly in love with you, Mark Brader," she murmurs against my lips. "Your mind is a gift. You're not broken." Her hand presses my side, over the place where my sweater hides my favorite word. "You're whole and complete, remember?"

She plants another kiss on my lips, and I want to lose myself in this moment. "It's finished," she whispers. "But we're not."

I pull her closer with one hand, the other brushing wind-tossed hair behind her ear.

She giggles and collapses against my chest, her arms looping around me. "Aren't you glad I saved your donuts? Do you still feel hogtied?"

"Caught and captured," I say while bending to pick up Lisa. "In the best way."

Nickie makes a silly face at the toddler, her eyes shining. "Sorry for ruining your plan again."

I grin and lean in close. "You were the best plan I never saw coming."

"You know what I think?"

"Not usually."

She presses her cheek to mine. "This is the best beginning."

# ACKNOWLEDGMENTS

"All this also comes from the Lord Almighty,
whose plan is wonderful,
whose wisdom is magnificent."
—Isaiah 28:29 NIV

Dear Reader,

My prayer before most writing sessions is that God grants me the talent to hook readers into a good story, to write through me, and that these books speak encouragement to the reader. May my words and thoughts and actions be pleasing in His sight as I write stories that point back to Him.

If you have dealt with anxiety in one form or another, I want to tell you that you are loved. You do not need to carry that burden by yourself.

Authors are interesting creatures. I've written half a million words through the eyes of people I made up in my head... but did I? Eloise, Tobias, Zeke, Hannah, Cordy, Gilbert, Nickie, Diana, Mark, Lauren... they are little pieces of you, and me, my friends, family, and neighbors. These characters teach me something new every day.

After I finish a book, I say, "Whew! That was exhausting. I'm done now. I don't need to ever do that again because it's way too much work." Then a little thing happens, like a car accident on the outskirts of Omaha. The flash of my white-tipped fingernails flying across my vision to protect my head from the impact repeats like a skipped CD I can't escape from.

And then God places a few more characters that walk around in my head. They are noisy. Thoughts of them consume me until I get them on paper.

So, here I am, book five, saying, "Whew! That was hard. I don't ever need to do that again. I'm done."

But... there are already some new and noisy characters pulling out chairs.

Mom, I officially dedicate this book to you because you never sit around and spout lies about "can't," and you sure never let us kids do it either. I love you.

Coaches Craig, Galel, Daniel, and Gavin with Early To Rise, thanks for the energy you share with everyone you come in contact with. The world is a better place because of you all.

Megan Schaulis, hey, hi, hello. Love you. Thanks for being my obsessive author friend and sending seven minute voice memos telling me all the things.

Mandi Blake, please write more Blackwater romance. We need to know what Dawson and Asa are up to.

To every single one of you still reading—you are a gift. Thank you for telling people about Hadley Springs and sharing this story of hope and humor.

Love,
Tasha

# ALSO BY TASHA HACKETT

## *Hearts of the Midwest*

### 1. *Bluebird on the Prairie*

In 1879, Nebraska, Eloise keeps house for her brother and nephew. She hides from the world—lost in grief for her husband who tragically died their first year of marriage.

Zeke is merely passing through on his way to California until he falls headfirst into a creek where Eloise is playing with little Luke in nothing but her unmentionables. *Gasp*

### 2. *Wildflower on the Prairie*

Hannah Benton is determined to escape the confines of her critical and controlling mother. The best way to obtain freedom is to get married! She has three months to find a husband... She can do it, but it sure doesn't leave time to dilly-dally.

## Holidays in Hadley Springs

### 1. *Waiting for Gilbert*

"I'm just a girl, standing in front of her phone, asking her landlord to come to dinner."

Cordy is ready to be serious and focused... who knew moving next door to the man of her dreams would be so distracting?

### 2. *Planning for Nickie*

"Fifty-three weeks is plenty of time to find a wife. One week to plan, fifty-two to execute."

Mark is ready to follow-through on the next step for his life goals... who knew a scrubs-wearing, donut-saving, sweet-smiling woman could derail his plans so efficiently?

***Kindergarten Math: Teach Me to Number My Days***

This 100 lesson course is designed specifically for the Christian homeschool family. It makes use of the Bible, a calendar, pencil and paper, counting bears, and pattern blocks, but there are no worksheets. It's a beautiful student-teacher conversation to look forward to each day.

Did you enjoy this story? Be sure to leave a review on your favorite platform and find Tasha online. Thank you for requesting these books at libraries and bookstores.

www.TashaHackett.com.

Tasha's still trying to decide what she wants to be when she grows up. In the meantime, she sings, paints, sews, dances in the kitchen, homeschools the kids, and often forgets to put away the laundry. Tasha writes with hope and humor to encourage and entertain. Her novels demonstrate a vision of romance between flawed characters loved by an unflawed God.